SEXY SCOT

HIGHLANDER'S THROUGH TIME

CECELIA MECCA

ALTIORA PRESS

SEXY SCOT Copyright © 2020 by Cecelia Mecca

Cover Design by Qamber Designs & Media

Corver Photography by Wander Aguiar

Edited by Angela Polidoro

Proofread by Carolina Vasquez

No part of this book may be reproduced in any form or by any electronic or mechanical means, including information storage and retrieval systems, without written permission from the author, except for the use of brief quotations in a book review.

This is a work of fiction. Characters, places and events, are either the products of the author's imagination or used in a fictitious manner. Any resemblance to actual persons, living or dead, or actual events is purely coincidental.

DEDICATION

As always, a huge thank you to Angela and Carolina as well as Elaine, Lorrie and Joanna for helping to make Sexy Scot perfect. I'd also like to thank Julie Johnstone for being an amazing writing partner and being so patient with my spreadsheet obsession.

1

———

Present Day

"Holy fuck."

Greyson and his brothers dropped the silver cross at the same time, the plush Persian rug in their father's study capturing its fall. Staring at it, and then each other, none of them spoke, all of them acutely aware of the empty space where their brother Rhys had been standing moments before. Even Ian was stunned into silence, a rarity for the youngest McCaim.

"What the hell just happened?" Reikart asked.

None of them had the answer. Rhys's disappearance was illogical. It should have been impossible. And yet, there was no disputing he was gone. Their big brother, the person who'd always held them together, had just disappeared on the final word of the ancient Gaelic chant none of them had thought would work.

"No." Greyson recoiled from the others, shaking his head. "No."

"Grey, he's gone," Ian said. Both he and Reikart were looking at Greyson expectantly, as if they thought he would know what to say. What to do.

But he had . . . nothing. Business was his expertise, not magic. He'd always thought their father's fixation with time travel and ancient Scotland was the product of a sick mind, an inability to cope with their mother's disappearance. He'd never imagined there might be something to it.

No, Rhys had to be here somewhere. Storming out of the study, he passed all the evidence of their father's obsession—stacks of ancient books, scattered papers, scrolls, and assorted artifacts—and burst out of the French doors. His brothers were already shouting after him, but he stayed focused on his mission, calling Rhys's name as he headed down the marble entranceway to the back doors, his pulse rising in tempo with his steps. He could hear his own voice becoming more and more desperate with each room he searched.

And there were plenty of them.

McCaim Shipping had been good to their family. But billions of dollars hadn't stopped their mother from disappearing. Nor had their fortune curbed their father's obsession with finding her. Now their father lay in a coma, and their brother had just disappeared into thin air. The McCaims had fallen apart. Expensive portraits, imported vases. They meant nothing.

Which was just as well since his baby brother, who'd followed him on his ill-fated trek through the house, hurled one of those vases against the hardwood floor, a temper tantrum better suited to a toddler than a twenty-seven-year-old man. Ian was only three years younger than Greyson, but it might as well have been a lifetime in terms of maturity. Reikart had followed him, his brow creased with worry.

Get a grip, Greyson. They need you to take charge. You're the next eldest. The heir apparent.

"Ian." He grabbed his brother's shoulder. "Ian."

But the fit of rage was over, another emotion following in its wake. Ian sat heavily in the hallway, tears running down his cheeks. Reikart didn't hesitate—he put his arms around him, holding him like a *wee babe*, as their mother would say. Greyson did the same.

"We *will* figure this out," he said, regaining the control that should never have left him. Time to accept the truth. He knew what had happened in that study. They could call Rhys's name all day, but he wasn't going to amble out of the guest suite or the bathroom. He was gone.

"How?" Reikart asked. "How will we figure this out, Grey?"

Damned if he knew. But he could guess.

"Dad was right."

Ian pushed them off, his large body easily breaking away from their grip. He hadn't been a football star for nothing. "Do you know what you're saying?" he asked, almost an accusation.

Greyson would give his little brother one thing, he didn't have a self-conscious bone in his body. Ian didn't give a shit that he'd just cried like a baby or tossed a $1,500 vase against the wall. Some days he wished he could be more like that. Right now, though, the last thing they needed was two temperamental McCaim brothers. Time to roll out his self-control and take command of the situation.

"I know exactly what I'm saying."

It was fucking insane—minutes ago he'd called this a "fantasy"—but he'd seen it happen with his own eyes. They all had. They couldn't keep pretending otherwise.

Standing, he held out a hand, and Ian grabbed hold of it. Greyson pulled his brother up and silently led the way back to the study. He got there first. The strange silver cross lay where it had fallen, and he made his way to it, compelled. It looked ancient, as if it were . . .

Hundreds of years old.

He knelt beside it, reaching out. Just as before, it was cold to the touch. More than cold—it gave him the sensation of being outside in a bracing wind—the feeling even stronger than it had been before. Lifting it, he turned toward Reikart and Ian.

"I can't believe I'm saying this, but it worked. There's no other explanation. You saw what I saw. Rhys disappeared. Which means Dad was right all along."

"Yeah." Ian shook his head. "That makes total sense. Mom didn't actually disappear five years ago. She time-traveled from the past before we were born and one day—*poof*—went back home. And now Rhys has gone back too. Poor bastard always wanted to go to medieval Scotland. Maybe he should have settled for a theme restaurant."

If Rhys were here, he'd have something to say about their brother's smart-ass tone. Greyson ignored it. He could understand Ian's anger. And Reikart's persistent look of disbelief. But they weren't really left with much of a choice here.

"Grey," Reikart said, trying to reason with him "You don't seriously believe that, do you?"

He didn't want to. And yet . . .

"What's the alternative?" Greyson demanded.

He waited for one of them to come up with something, hoping it would happen. But he already knew better. There was no disputing the facts. Their father had slipped into a coma, and they'd come to his study to search for clues about their mother's disappearance. What they'd found was this silver cross and a chant in an ancient tongue. On Rhys's insistence, they'd held the cross and recited the chant, and Rhys had disappeared.

Disappeared.

It was absolutely crazy. Insane. But it had also happened.

They'd all thought their father had gone off the deep end—so much so that Rhys and Greyson had taken control of their family business. But this meant he wasn't crazy after all. This meant their mother might actually be from thirteenth-century Scotland.

His brothers were still looking at him expectantly, hoping he could pull answers out of his ass, but he had none to give them. It was more pressure than he'd ever felt while making a business deal.

"We're going to try it again."

Both Reikart and Ian erupted at once. He immediately cut them off.

"We're going to try it again, and this time we all go back."

"Pfft. Back through time, you mean?" Ian was clearly still in denial.

"Didn't we try to do just that?" Reikart asked. "But Rhys is gone, and we're still here." He had not said *dumbass*, but his look said it. "What makes you think the result will be different this time?"

Greyson glared, but his brother was right. Something had gone wrong last time, which meant they needed a contingency plan.

"If only one or two of us get through, whoever's left behind has to keep trying."

The contingency plan was shit, but it was all they had. Greyson pretended he wasn't absolutely terrified.

Neither of his brothers looked convinced.

No one said aloud what he was sure all three of them were thinking. Rhys and their mother could both be dead. Did it kill you, traveling through time? Who the hell knew, when it wasn't supposed to be possible in the first place. They were dealing with dozens of big, fat unknowns here.

The stress of all those unknowns had nearly destroyed their father, a man so determined and driven he'd built a billion-dollar shipping company from one ship he'd spent his life savings to purchase.

"Mom. Rhys. They could be in trouble."

And that was all it took. With those five words, his brothers reached out to touch the Celtic cross he still held. They turned as one to look at the chant Rhys had tacked to the wall, scribbled on a piece of scrap paper. It meant nothing to him, but Rhys had thought the words significant. They read them together, slowly, carefully, Greyson's sheer will keeping his hands from shaking.

"*Talamh, èadhar, teine, usige ga thilleadh dhachaigh.*"

2

September 1286

MARIAN SAT ATOP HER HORSE, staring back at the keep, the only home she had known for four and twenty years. Her father hadn't deemed it necessary to appear in the courtyard for a final fare-thee-well, but Gilda had made up for his oversight, as was her custom, though the maid's tears were not a welcome sight. They only reminded Marian she would likely never see the woman who had raised her again.

They had hugged, and cried, and hugged again. Finally, she'd given into the inevitable and mounted her horse. Nothing to do but wave farewell to the elderly woman. If she thought it would do any good, she would rush back into the hall and beg her father once again to allow the maid to accompany her north. But he would not allow her that simple kindness any more than he would agree to halt her wedding. He'd made it clear both decisions were his and his alone.

"Are you prepared to take your leave, my lady?" James asked.

The marshal felt poorly for her, she could tell, but the kindly knight's sentiment would not help her. Not today.

"Aye." She urged her mount forward. Waving goodbye one last time to the small crowd that had gathered, Gilda at the front, Marian followed the small riding party forward. A cold fall breeze urged Marian to pull the fur-lined mantle more tightly around her shoulders.

It wasn't until they passed through the massive gatehouse that her father's man spoke again.

"Your father is right. She'd not have made the journey easily," James said, falling in line next to her.

"'Tis just as well." Marian offered the marshal the largest smile she was able to manage under the circumstances. "Duncan's reputation precedes him. She is likely safer here."

James said nothing to that. They both knew she was correct in that particular assessment. The Earl of Fife was vengeful and philandering, and gossip had it his son, her intended, was much the same. Even so, Gilda had wanted to accompany her. Marian had tried to dissuade her at first, but Gilda had refused to acknowledge her resistance. And once she had warmed to the idea of having at least one familiar face in her new home, the idea had become a beacon in her dark future.

Until her father had smothered it.

Contradicting herself, she muttered aloud, "I just don't believe him. I don't believe he cares for Gilda's health."

James said nothing for a moment. She had become accustomed to the marshal's silence, knowing he defaulted to it in lieu of speaking ill of his master. But then he surprised her by asking the same question Marian had posed to her many times in the past weeks.

"What could have been the real reason for his denial?"

He spoke more freely than normal.

Ahhh. Because he knew her father would never learn of it.

Her new life was to be in Scotland. If she ever returned to this castle, it would be years from now.

The thought of what those long years might hold for her pressed in on her, but soft golden light spilled down on them, dispelling the worst of her mood.

"Look!" Marian pointed to the sun emerging from a bed of clouds. "'Tis certainly a May Day miracle."

James and the others who rode within earshot looked up to the lovely sight, which was indeed rare for this time of year.

"Mayhap God is smiling down on this new beginning for me."

Aware the others looked at her strangely, Marian attempted to rein in the *overwhelming optimism* she had long been accused of by her father. "Or mayhap 'tis naught but the sun deciding to make an appearance for the first time in months."

But James was already shaking his head. "I believe your first assessment correct, my lady," he said kindly. "'Tis very possible your betrothed is a better man than his reputation suggests."

She ignored the snickering from the riders in front of them and chose to play along. "Perhaps you are right. For all we know, Duncan is a handsome, kind, loyal . . ." She stopped, realizing how silly the words sounded. "I'm not fool enough to believe all of the horrifying things said of our northern neighbors, but perhaps you can allay some of my lingering fears on the matter."

Marian did not care for his expression.

"Surely they are not all as bad as that?"

She had met more than one Scotsman in her day, and they seemed very much like her own countrymen. But James's bearded face was contorted in a way that made her shudder.

"Of course they are not, my lady . . ."

He didn't expand on that comment, and Marian understood why. They weren't speaking of just any Scotsman, but a very particular one. A very particular family. And while the Earl of Fife may be an important man, one of the newly appointed Guardians of Scotland, if the rumors proved correct, neither he nor his son had much to recommend them beyond their wealth and power.

She had known this day was coming. But the future that had felt so distant in Fenwall was soon to become her reality—in just one sennight, she would be a woman wed. She would give anything to avoid her fate, to be in control of her own future, but wishing for such things was childish. It could no more save her from this marriage than it could bring her mother back to life.

"I am to be married," she said softly, as if saying it aloud would help her come to peace with it.

"Aye, my lady, you are," James said. "And I am sorry for it."

"Do not be sorry. Such is the way of things."

She lifted a hand to the chain inside her mantle, needing the reassurance of it—and came up empty. We must go back." She searched the marshal's face frantically. "We must go back. I forgot my chain. James, we must go back."

She didn't need to explain herself further. He knew what she meant as well as she did. It was one of the few things she possessed that had belonged to the mother who had died giving birth to her.

"I placed it next to my bed so I would remember it."

Marian ignored the men's laughter. Everyone from Fenwall knew of her forgetfulness. Nearly every day she forgot something, or someone—just the day before, she attempted to leave the keep without a mantle.

"We must go back."

But she knew from James's expression, though he uttered not a word, they would not be going back. Her father would rage if they did.

For the first time that day, she allowed her anger and resentment and fear to surface. She hated for the men to see her upset. But if she could have chosen one thing to take to Scotland, other than her beloved maid, it would have been her mother's chain.

Appropriate, she supposed, casting her gaze up to the others, that it would be left behind.

3

THE CHANTING HADN'T WORKED. Although the cross had continued to pulse cold into their hands, nothing had happened. They'd stood around looking stupid for a minute, then tried three times more. Still nothing. They'd taken tequila shots and proceeded to comb through the debris in their father's office, hoping to find something revelatory. A few days later, they were still looking. They'd fallen into a new routine: spending their days covering for Rhys and running the company, their nights attempting to crack the code.

In the moments in between, they went to see their father in shifts. Grey was just returning from one such visit now: their dad didn't seem any better, but he didn't seem any worse either. He could still wake up from the coma, or so the doctors said.

A text from Ian dinged on his phone.

Go around back. Reporters.

Grey cursed under his breath. It had only been a matter of time before the reporters found out about their father.

"Around the back," he told his driver. "Reporters." Although he'd always resisted having a driver, he'd been serving as the fill-in CEO in his brother's absence. A driver was a must. His mind would have been on overdrive even without the added stress of the time travel debacle. Being second-born was a bitch, especially with an older brother who was basically God, at least in the eyes of their father. And the shareholders. And who was he kidding? Everyone saw Rhys that way, Greyson included. And he wouldn't rest until he got his brother back.

Before the car had even stopped at the back entrance of the mansion, he was up and out. He made his way through the door, hurrying to his father's study. The rest of the house was pristine. Deep hardwood contrasted with white walls and pillars, including the one on which Ian had once drawn his name in pink chalk. Greyson would have smiled at the memory if his life, their lives, hadn't gone completely to shit four days ago.

"Finally," Reikart muttered as he entered the study.

Ian had already poured out a round of tequila shots, part of the nightly ritual they'd established. In his little brother's eyes, it would be bad luck not to continue it—he'd always been the most superstitious of the four of them, which made it surprising he was the only one still fighting the truth. Reikart had accepted it as he did everything, with an easy air, but Greyson suspected a storm brewed under the mask his brother showed the world. Downing his shot, Greyson looked at the black leather book in Ian's hands.

"Anything new?"

According to his father's notes, that book, some kind of ancient Scottish spellbook, was the key to unraveling the mystery of time travel. From what their mother had told him, her sister, Grace, had accidentally sent her from thirteenth-century Scotland, at some place called Castle Kinghorn, to New Orleans. Mom had come through more than thirty-five years ago, when she was just twenty-one. But Dad had never gotten the chant to work for him, and although they'd seen Rhys disappear, they couldn't get it to work for them either. Ian, although still skeptical, had suggested it might have something to do with the wording, but unfortunately only one of them had learned Gaelic. And that someone had disappeared before their eyes four nights ago, here, in this very spot. They'd tried looking up pronunciations on Google, but it hadn't helped. If anything, it had made them worse.

"I wish I hadn't chosen archery," he muttered. "Damned useless." Their mother had insisted each of the boys learn something from her homeland—leave it to Rhys to choose the hardest skill to master.

Reikart poured a second shot for himself and downed it before collecting their glasses. The storm surge must be growing.

"Nothing new," Ian finally responded. "Unless you count the new regulation for filing Sea Cargo Manifest in India. I'm starting to think this book's as useless as your bows and arrows."

Ian shot his brother a look, but the unrepentant bastard just shrugged his shoulders. He could be a smart-ass for sure, but Ian could recite shipping regulations in his sleep.

"We need to get him back." Reikart stared at the cross, which they'd set on the desk. "First Dad. Now this. That leaves only three of us and too much work." He jerked a hand through his hair and added, "McCaim can only hold out for so long." What he didn't say—but what Greyson heard—was, *We can only hold out for so long.*

"Keeping the business afloat is the least of our concerns," Greyson said, reaching for the cross. But even as he said it, he knew it wasn't quite true. Finding out what the hell had happened to their mother and Rhys, getting their father to wake up from his terrifying slumber, and fending off jittery shareholders . . . all of it was their concern.

Uneasy lies the head that wears a crown.

Quoting Shakespeare was another useless skill. Maybe

instead of minoring in British literature he should have taken some courses in time travel and other impossible ventures.

"Let's do it," he said, glancing at each of his brothers in turn. Cold was rolling through him from his grip on the cross.

He ignored Ian's eye roll—the boy had popped out of their mother's womb rolling his eyes at all three of them. But not at Mom. She'd have given him the ass-whooping he deserved just for attempting it.

With a quick glance at the maps next to his brother's note, the ones they'd been studying for the past four days—one of Perthshire, Scotland, their mother's homeland, and another depicting the border between England and Scotland—he nodded for them to begin.

At least now they knew what they were saying. Earth, air, fire, water, return him home.

"*Talamh, èadhar, teine, usige ga thilleadh dhachaigh.*"

Nothing.

"*Talamh, èadhar, teine, usige ga thilleadh dhachaigh,*" *they said in unison again.*

Something clicked in Greyson's head, and a voice whispered in his ear: *Say it like Rhys.*

As if a video were playing in his head, Greyson saw and heard Rhys say the words, and he chanted with him.

"*Talamh, èadhar, teine, usige ga thilleadh dhachaigh.*"

It was as if lightning had struck the cross, jolting it away from his hands. Everything went black. Greyson couldn't see a thing except for a single bright light, but it felt like he was floating above his body, like he imagined happened when someone died. He could smell stale beer and hay, and loud, incomprehensible voices rang in his ears. A boot nudged his ribs, soft at first but then harder. He wanted to lash out but couldn't move any part of his body. Except his heart. It pounded in his chest and in his ears, the sound competing with the shouts. One in particular stood out.

The words finally registered: "Get outta the way."

Another kick.

This time, Greyson was able to push away the boot that kicked at his side.

"Ye're blockin' the door."

He swallowed, his throat on fire from the effort, and managed to push up on all fours. Shook his head in an attempt to clear it.

"What in the name of the king is he wearing?"

They were talking about him. A young girl with curly brown hair and a cherublike face stared at him. Specifically, at the scar on his right jaw courtesy of an archery mishap in college. Blinking, Greyson opened his eyes and looked straight into another face, one of a fearsome-looking Viking. He'd always been fascinated by the Vikings, and this guy looked like he'd literally stepped out of a documentary. Wearing a mixture of leather and plated armor, a freaking massive sword hanging by his side, he was a behemoth of a man. And most definitely not from his time.

His time. As in, a different time than this one.

With his wits finally returning, he looked around the room frantically. No sign of his younger brothers.

"A reiver?" someone asked.

"Nay," another answered.

A crowd began to gather, which was the exact opposite of what he needed right now. Greyson scrambled to his feet and made his way to the door. He opened it, and the sunlight blinded him, the darkness of the bar, or tavern, or whatever, not preparing him for the fact that it was the middle of the day. Looking up to the creaking above him, he saw a wooden sign swaying back and forth. No words, just two images: a rabbit and a cross.

"Ye're a poor sight, lad."

The man who'd kicked him had apparently followed him outside.

Greyson had spent the last few sleepless nights imagining what would happen if it actually worked, if he and his brothers managed to transport themselves back through time. What would it feel like? Would he survive the journey? How would he acclimate? How would he find his way around?

But not one of those considerations had prepared him for the reality of waking up in what was apparently medieval Scotland. And none of the feeble excuses he'd come up with seemed viable now that he was staring down a real-life frigging warrior.

"I . . ." What the hell could he possibly say? "Where am I?"

At least he hadn't asked, *What year is this?* He'd promised himself not to do that. It was a sure ticket to crazy town, and if Greyson knew anything about this time period, which was admittedly limited to what he'd learned in the past few days, it was that they didn't deal well with mental illness. And they'd presume the worst of him if he spoke even a portion of his new truth.

The Viking didn't answer.

Greyson realized the man wasn't actually a Viking, but from his attire to his long, dirty-blond hair pulled back with a leather strap and bushy, blond-brown beard, he very much looked the part.

"Ross." Another Viking stumbled out the door. Nay, this one looked less like a Viking and more like a medieval cosplayer. "Who the hell is he?"

Receiving no immediate response, the drunken cosplayer quickly lost interest and staggered away.

"Come with me," the first man, Ross, said.

As if Greyson had a choice. Ross grabbed him by the arm with a viselike grip that put Ian's wrestling moves to shame. And Ian, despite being the baby of the family, was no shrinking violet. Neither was he, a fact that hardly seemed to matter at the moment.

"From where do you hail?" Ross asked.

Although the shutters were closed, they could still hear the interested shouts and murmurs from inside the tavern.

The truth would not do. Greyson had to think of something to say, preferably sooner rather than later.

"You've a strange accent," the man continued.

This he knew for certain, but he had no real answer for it. "I'm Scottish," he said truthfully.

The Viking's laugh caught him off guard.

"You're no more Scotsman than the Cony and Cross's innkeeper."

Was that supposed to make any sense?

"Both my parents are Scottish," he said lamely, the whole time-traveling thing scrambling his brain.

Think, Greyson. Think.

"Shona MacKinnish—"

The words barely left his mouth before Ross the Viking grabbed his tie, using it to haul him forward. He handled him as if Greyson weren't just over six feet, his frame no less honed than Rhys's, thanks to punishing hours at the gym.

"You're acquainted with Shona MacKinnish?"

Good. If the Viking knew his mother, perhaps he also knew where to find her.

"She's my mother."

A murderous expression crossed the man's face. But Greyson had not survived being hurled through time straight into the Middle Ages just so his skull could be crushed by this big brute of a man. No way was he giving the Viking time to go for that sword. Not before he found his mother and brother.

Grabbing the big man's wrist, Greyson twisted, the howl of pain a welcome sound to his ears.

"Kick me or touch me again. I dare you." He pushed the

Viking away with a hard enough shove that his back bounced off the front wall of the tavern.

Ross reached for his sword.

"I don't think so."

This time, it was his hands that wrapped around the Viking's neck. Adrenaline coursed through him. It was the only possible explanation for how easily he was holding the much larger man at bay. If only he'd thought to bring a weapon . . . or wear something less conspicuous than a suit. Ian had even joked about it, asking if they should dress the part before attempting to time-travel again. Unfortunately, deep down, none of them had really thought it would work. Reikart had admitted as much the day before.

"I mean Shona MacKinnish no harm," Greyson conceded.

When the Viking loosened himself from Greyson's grasp, he proved that an ironfisted punch to the gut felt about the same in the thirteenth century as it did in the twenty-first. Thankfully, he'd sparred enough with Rhys, who'd taken up boxing as well as Gaelic, to shrug it off easily enough. Jumping back to his feet, prepared to take or make another punch, he was stopped by the sound of steel.

The Viking had pulled out his sword much more quickly than Greyson would have expected for a man that size. For a sword that size.

Fantastic.

An undershirt, shirt, and tie wouldn't do anything to shield his chest from the tip of the massive sword resting just over his heart.

"Who are you?" Ross said on a growl.

Hearing his mother's name had clearly pissed this guy off. But he had nothing to offer him but the truth. Or part of it, at least.

"My name is Greyson McCaim." While in the Middle Ages, might as well talk like someone in the Middle Ages—or try. His frame of reference wasn't much larger than a few TV shows he'd watched. "Son of Colin McCaim and Shona MacKinnish." He was pretty sure the sword had just punctured his flesh.

Never in his wildest dreams had he imagined dying this way. Caught in the crosshairs of a gunman in the Quarter while out carousing with his drunken brothers? Maybe. But not like this.

"And I can prove it," he blurted.

His plan was risky. Beyond risky. Given the medieval fear of witchcraft, he was just as likely to be killed for showing the Viking his cellphone as he was for identifying himself as Shona's son. But he was running out of options.

"I'm waiting," the Viking grumbled, clearly comfortable with his position of power.

"I'm going to grab something in my pocket. It's just a . . ."

A what? Cellphone? Picture? Jesus.

"A small black box with a drawing inside. A drawing of my mother. Of Shona."

Thank you, Reikart.

At least one of them had had the presence of mind to insist they all take pictures. Lots of them. Of the maps. Of their mother's note. Of every damn thing in their father's study.

Slowly, carefully, he pulled the phone out of his pocket. In a moment of sheer panic, Greyson realized it might not even work. Who knew what time travel did to a cell battery? But when he pressed the button, the phone glowed to life and the Viking nearly dropped his damn sword.

If only.

Ross stared at the screen in shock, clearly afraid of the device. Reaching below the sharp edge of the sword, Greyson swiped frantically, his heart beating almost as heavily as when he'd first found himself on the tavern floor.

"Here," he said. "My mother."

He turned the phone around, showing the brute the

youngest picture of his mom they could find in the study. Watching his eyes widen, Greyson went in for the kill.

"And this is a note she wrote. In her own handwriting. I took a picture of it before . . ."

His eyes caught the Viking's. Ice blue. Like his mother's.

"A . . ."

"Picture. Like a drawing. See, she wrote this note."

One minute, the sword pressed against his chest. The next, it dropped, the Viking snatching the phone from his hand.

"You can swipe. Like this."

Back and forth, he showed him the image and the note, careful not to go the wrong way. Lord knew what the next pictures were.

"Shona."

His voice, barely a whisper, held something Greyson had missed earlier. This man didn't just know his mother. He knew her well. Was he . . . ?

"'Tis my sister. That . . . drawing . . . is of my sister."

Greyson's mouth dropped open.

The Viking looked up, his head shaking in disbelief. "God's nails, Grace, you really did it."

Grace. Was that . . . was he talking about his aunt? The one he'd only learned about this week. The one who was apparently responsible for his mother's trip through time. So much for his mom being an orphan. But this finally explained her Scottish accent.

"Where are you from?" the Viking asked, although his tone was more civil.

"I . . ."

He still had no answers to give. New Orleans would mean nothing to this man.

"You're from the future?"

The Viking shoved Greyson's phone back at him before he

could answer. Before he could even shut his gaping mouth. "Put it away. Never show it to anyone else. Do you understand?"

Greyson did as he was told, and quite happily. Because the Viking, apparently also his uncle, no longer seemed inclined to kill him.

"She really did it," the big man murmured under his breath. "Grace isn't mad."

Mad meant crazy, didn't it? He had an inkling of what was happening here. "She sent her, my mother, didn't she? Grace sent my mother to the future?"

This time, the Viking looked at him as if he were an alien. Which, he supposed, was kind of accurate. But then the man sheathed his sword and stuck out his hand. Another gesture that apparently transcended time.

"Ross MacKinnish, brother to Shona MacKinnish." A quick glance around, as if to ensure they were indeed alone, and he added, "Well met, nephew."

Yeah, not so well met. But Greyson would let that one slide.

Shaking his hand, he said, "Pleased to meet you. Maybe now you can tell me where we are. And where my mother is. And maybe you've seen her other son, my brother Rhys?"

But he could tell from Ross's expression that he had no idea what he was talking about.

"We're in England. Just south of the Scottish border. I've not seen your brother, and as for Shona, you're going to help me find her."

Help me find her.

So she was still lost. Greyson swallowed.

"But not"—Ross nodded toward Greyson's suit—"in that."

PRIOR TO THE JOURNEY, Marian had wondered at her father's decision to send her off with such a small riding party. Gilda, who'd always attempted to persuade her that her father did, indeed, care about her, had simply shrugged and said, "He must know 'tis a safe path from Fenwall to Pittillock." She'd managed to say it with a straight face, although they both knew such a thing could not be true. The borderlands had become more dangerous than ever of late. "Or perhaps he trusts Sir James to keep you safe."

And, indeed, Sir James was quite protective. Whenever they came near any other travelers, the marshal would instantly fall in beside her. However, he'd developed a cough these last days, and she worried about his ruddy appearance. Her concern for him was undercut by her worry about the riding party that had just come into view ahead of them. There appeared to be at least six riders to their own twelve. But these were no ordinary men. Each one of them sat taller than all of her own companions save Big John. None of the riders had glanced back, which struck her as odd. Did they not hear them coming?

Did they simply not care?

"Scotsmen," James muttered, falling in line beside her once again.

Would Duncan be a protective husband? Likely not, if even a fraction of the gossip were true.

"Stay close, my lady."

The party ahead of them had slowed to a crawl, their leader stopping to dismount. Apparently they'd seen them after all. He did turn toward them now, and Marian shuddered. A more fearsome-looking man certainly did not exist in her country, or his.

"Well met," James called to them. Their group slowed too, the rest of the men falling in around Marian while James rode ahead, coming to a stop next to the blond, bearded man. She couldn't hear their words from such a distance, but the men appeared friendly enough. None made a move toward them, and her own men appeared relaxed enough. She'd begun to sense the difference between friend and foe, and from all appearances, these Scotsmen fell into the former group.

With her mount dancing impatiently under her, Marian reached out a hand to steady the mare—which was when she felt herself being watched. Inching forward, she turned toward the man. Immediately flooded with warmth, Marian shivered for a very different reason than before.

He was unlike any man Marian had ever seen. His hair, most unusual. Shorter on the sides than the top, raven black, it was a striking contrast to the cream of his shirt. His jaw firm, set in its assessment of her, the man neither smiled nor frowned. He simply stared at her with such intensity she had no choice but to continue watching him.

Marian simply could not look away.

Nearly as large as their leader, he sat atop his mount as if he were the former king's heir, though, of course, Alexander had none. What manner of man stared so openly, so boldly?

What manner of woman am I to hold his gaze?

Marian forced herself to shift her gaze to James and the leader. But the men who flanked her were moving away, the mood lightening, and she found herself tightening her grip on the reins and peeking.

Her mouth dropped. He was still staring.

Perhaps they were no threat, but this man's behavior marked them as heathens, her father's favorite word for the Scots. Of course, she'd pointed out he'd chosen to marry her to one of them for the sake of an alliance. He'd merely scoffed and turned away.

If they were closer, Marian might have admonished this man for his poor manners.

And then, as if his behavior weren't inappropriate enough, the man smiled at her. A slow, sensual smile that held promises which would be left unfulfilled. The kind of smile that might be given to a servant but never a noblewoman. But try as Marian might, she could not seem to turn away.

"Lady Marian?"

James called her name much too loudly, as if he'd been attempting to gain her attention for some time. With a deep, steadying breath, Marian cleared her throat and took his cue, spurring her mount forward.

The Scotsman watched them as they passed, their kindly faces not what she would have expected from such men.

She would not look back at the handsome rogue. She would not. But an itch to do so swept over her, compelling her attention. Maybe just a quick glance? What harm could that bring?

Sucking in a fortifying breath, Marian looked back over her shoulder and gasped.

Had he just *winked* at her? If her father had been here to see it, he would have challenged the Scotsman for such an action. His honor would have demanded it, not any protectiveness for his daughter.

IT WAS a bad idea to flirt with a lady—a real medieval lady—and yet Greyson couldn't help himself. He'd never seen anyone lovelier, and his mind was still racing from everything he'd learned in the past day and a half. Once Ross had accepted the fact that they were, implausibly enough, uncle and nephew, he'd brought Greyson to a secluded corner and told him what he knew of the strange tale in which they were both enmeshed. First, though, he took a long swig of ale that would have made Ian proud to call him uncle.

"My brother Colban and I were at our family home, at Castle Hightower, when Grace comes running through the courtyard as if someone was chasing her, screaming for Shona. Your aunt Grace has always been . . . different. Some even called her "ban-draoidh," but Grace is no witch, just a very skilled healer. She and your mother had been at Castle Kinghorn serving Queen Yolande as ladies-in-waiting."

"Mom served the queen?" he'd asked. His uncle had already told him the MacKinnishes were allied with Robert the Bruce. Of course, Greyson's mind had immediately jumped to the future king of Scotland, but further conversation had revealed this Bruce was the future king's grandfather.

"Aye, lad. Clan MacKinnish is as well-positioned as any in Scotland, courtesy of our father. Your grandfather. 'Tis a tale for another day. And I'm sorry to say the tale Grace spun was one I could not believe. She told us that Shona had been asked by Deidre Irvine, the queen's head lady-in-waiting, to deliver a message to King Alexander at Edinburgh Castle, asking for him to come immediately. As she returned to Kinghorn with the king, Yearger Irvine—Deidre's brother and one of Shona's escorts—apparently attempted to stab her. She escaped his clutches only to witness the other two guards in their riding party, Nigel, along with another guard named Loxton, scare the king's horse off the cliff."

"They killed him?" Greyson had been stunned by the news.

"Aye, they killed the king. And your mother delivered the message."

Greyson, who'd taken a liking to his uncle after their less than convivial introduction, had immediately turned defensive. "You didn't believe she was innocent?"

But Ross was already shaking his head. "'Twas not the part of the tale I didna believe. According to Grace, Shona made her way back to Kinghorn, went straight to the healing room to see Grace, and told her what had happened. When Deidre and Yearger came for Shona, Grace said she had no choice but to act quickly. Pulling out a cross given to her by the fae—"

"Fae? As in, fairies?"

Judging by his uncle's rather intimidating frown, he gathered the word *fairy* hadn't been invented yet. He wanted to ask more about the fae—what they looked like and if they were smaller than "normal" people—but he'd already been exposed to enough of the impossible. So he waved for his uncle to go on.

"Grace claimed to have grabbed the cross and said the words given to her by her fae friends, sending your mother, well, she thought back to Hightower. After she discovered your mother wasn't there, Grace kept repeating over and over, 'I did it wrong.' None knew what she meant, but we did know the king was dead. And Shona was missing."

"So when I showed up . . ."

Hearing the other side of the story had helped put the events in Greyson's time into context. He told his uncle about the cross, and the way the stories fit together had made it impossible for either of them to deny the truth. Grace had accidently sent his mother through time rather than back to Hightower. But knowing that did nothing to answer the shitload of questions they both had.

Where had Grace gotten another cross to pull his mom back through time, if indeed that's what had happened when she'd disappeared five years ago? And most importantly, how exactly was it possible to time travel? Because, scientifically, it couldn't be done. He'd spent several sleepless hours researching it after Rhys had vanished in their father's study.

In the end, it didn't matter how it had happened, only that it had. The so-called "traveling chant" somehow actually worked. And neither Greyson nor Ross believed he'd been plopped nearly into his uncle's lap by happenstance. If he hadn't believed in fate before, Greyson was quickly changing his opinion on the matter. Perhaps his mother had been meant to come to New Orleans. With luck, maybe Rhys had also ended up in a time and place that made some lick of sense.

Because, according to his uncle, who'd volunteered to bring a message south from the so-called "Guardians of Scotland" to the English king's regent, his mom's life had been threatened before she disappeared. And the cause of that threat was a man named Yearger Ross intended to question. Greyson had agreed to accompany him to deliver the message in the hopes of learning more about the whereabouts of his mother and Rhys.

Not that he had much of a choice. And if what Ross told him were true, they'd be doing more than talking to this Yearger character.

Greyson had never had more on his mind, so why, as the lovely lady rode in front of him, did he find himself wondering if perhaps they'd come across her for a reason too?

5

PARTLY LISTENING to the men's chatter as they headed to Quinting Castle, where King Edward's regent was currently holding court, Marian attempted to slow her rapidly beating heart.

Another coughing fit from James pulled her out of her reverie. In truth, the marshal did not appear as hardy as normal. Concern prompted her forward . . . and then she noticed them.

Not again.

This time the party rode toward them. At least ten men traversed the wooden bridge they'd crossed before turning south. Unlike the Scotsmen they'd just passed, these men had an entirely different air about them. Dressed very differently than her men or the Scotsmen, their horses smaller than normal, something was not quite right with these men. Even as she thought it, Marian found herself surrounded.

"Fenwall!" one of the newcomers shouted as they thundered toward them.

"Lady Marian, to the trees." That was James's voice, in a pitch she'd never heard before. Angry and panicked. She had no time to respond before he urged her horse forward, into the thick woods beside them. Pine needles scratched her cheek as her spooked mount veered too close to wayward branches.

Stopping to look back at the racket of shouts and clanging metal, Marian stared in shock at the sight behind her. From this distance, all she could see were men grappling. Her father's men were being attacked. Or were they doing the attacking? She could not be sure, but James had wanted her to escape. To hide. A surge of strength flooded her, and she rode away from the action again, moving as fast as she dared over the uneven ground, only to find a different sort of danger in front of her.

No. No, no, no.

She could see the water through the trees, but she kept riding toward it, hoping to find some escape. But the lake stretched out in front of her in both directions, its stillness so at odds with the screams that continued to ring in her ears that Marian had difficulty reconciling it. The water lay as smooth as the glass-paned windows of which her father was so proud. Only the wealthiest could afford such a luxury, he'd boasted.

Her father. The same man who so adamantly refused to train her. Training that could have proved quite useful at this moment.

There was no way around it, but mayhap she would swim across.

The bank across from her beckoned as she sat atop her horse, immobile.

Too far. Too cold. She could swim, but even if she made it, she might die from cold. And while she could ride along the bank, she was uncertain about which way to go.

She only knew she could not go back.

Into the woods, James had said.

But if she stayed atop her horse, she would surely be seen. The men wouldn't have to ride far to find her. Dismounting and praying she made the right decision, Marian gave a final soulful look to her faithful horse. And ran.

Back into the woods, but south. At least she thought it was south. It was so difficult to discern in here. But did it matter, really? Marian was alone without a weapon.

And someone was coming.

She would die this day.

Hiding as best she could in a thicket of bushes, she cursed herself for a fool. Why had she not kept riding? Although she could hide better on foot, she would not be able to run from an attacker.

The surge of strength from earlier had faded, leaving in its wake a dread worse than what she'd felt upon learning of her betrothal. Mayhap this would be a quick death, unlike the promise of a slow one as Duncan's wife.

Nay, I will not simply wait for death.

Her hiding spot, as sound as any, would protect her until James returned. As skilled and strong as any knight, he'd served her father well, was chosen as marshal for a reason. He *would* come for her.

Someone shouted her name, surely one of her own men? But the voice sounded foreign to her ears. Balling her hands into fists to attempt to stop them from shaking, Marian crouched even lower, cursing the bright blue of her riding gown.

"Marian?"

Another shout, but surely it was not one of her men. None would call her by her given name.

God, please save me. I promise to be less foolish and happy, and act more like a lady. I will serve my new husband as a wife should.

Shame washed over her. She was about to die, and here she sat, lying to God.

Nay, God, I shall not lie to you.

Too many times I've attempted to be the kind of woman who would make my father proud, and too many times I've failed. I fear 'tis not possible. But I do promise to serve Duncan well, or as best as possible given my temperament.

Still, it felt like a promise she might not be able to keep.

Allow me to live, and I promise to temper my unkind thoughts of the Scotsman.

Surely she could manage that much.

"Marian."

He was much too close. Marian didn't intend to shift, but she did, and the snapped branch echoed as loudly as the first clang of metal in the attack on the road. This time, there was no stopping her hands from shaking. She was losing control of her body as it warred against her, urging her to release the muscles she tensed. Biting the insides of her lip to keep herself from making a sound, she continued to remain still.

"Marian?"

The man had heard the branch and was coming closer.

She would fight. Marian would not die without at least attempting to overpower him. Intending to do just that, she lunged at the sound of footsteps just beyond her hiding spot.

And tripped on the hem of her gown, falling. She anticipated the pain of hitting the ground, but a pair of strong arms caught her instead. She looked up and gasped, surprised to find herself staring into the very last eyes she'd expected to see.

6

GREYSON RUSHED FORWARD and caught her just in time.

Hands still shaking from what had just happened, nearly overwhelmed with relief that he'd found her alive, he did the only thing that seemed logical. Pulling her against him, Greyson wrapped his arms around her, though for whose comfort he wasn't sure.

He could sense her pulling back at first, but just when he loosened his grip, the Englishwoman held on to him for dear life. He could feel her sobs against his chest, and though it usually made him feel useless and uncomfortable when a woman cried in front of him, Greyson had no desire to release her. He understood it, the overwhelming flood of emotion.

I just killed a man. Maybe two of them.

Countless hours of hitting targets, first in high school and then in college, and never in his wildest dreams had he imagined he might one day use a bow and arrow to kill a human being. His uncle's pleasure at learning Greyson was proficient in archery, though certainly not with such a rudimentary crossbow as the one they'd purchased in one of the villages they'd passed through . . . well, he understood it now. Less than two days here, and he'd already seen his first battle. Ross had warned him, but he never imagined it to come so soon.

"What . . ." Shoulders heaving up and down, she didn't seem inclined to finish, so Greyson answered her unasked question.

"We came upon—" He cut himself off before he could say *slaughter*. Jesus, she was in for a shock. "Your men were under attack."

For the first time since he'd so impulsively embraced her, Greyson pulled back. Her cheeks, so perfectly flawless earlier, were now splotchy with tears. Her vulnerability, so evident, made him forget about his own predicament. And she still had no idea what awaited her back on the road.

"We saw it happen, so we came forward to help."

Reaching down inside her coat—no, Uncle Ross had called it a mantle—she took out a handkerchief. A cotton one, the embroidery so fine no one in his century would dare to actually use it. Wiping her cheeks as prettily as if she were taking afternoon tea and not standing with a stranger in the middle of the woods, she backed away from him. It struck him that she seemed embarrassed.

"We saw them riding toward us in the distance," she said. "So fast. James told me to run—" Her eyes widened. "Sir James. Is he well? He is the strongest of knights but has been unwell as of late. Please tell me he is unharmed?"

Shit.

"He is, I mean, your men . . ." Since when did he fumble for words? Since never. But how exactly did a man go about telling a woman her entire riding party was dead? In his time, it would be called a massacre, but his uncle had shrugged it off as if a slew of dead bodies were an everyday occurrence.

Probably because it *was* an everyday occurrence here.

Double shit. He was in way over his head.

"I can walk you back," he said lamely.

"Your speech. 'Tis quite odd."

If only she knew.

"Where are you from?"

Did the U.S. even exist now? He might have gone to Yale, but Greyson had never been great with remembering dates—it was the only part of his English minor he'd struggled to master.

"Abroad."

Apparently the word was pretty odd. Her brows furrowed, drawing his attention. Like every other feature on her face, their expressiveness captivated him. Just like when she'd ridden past him earlier. Everything about this woman pulled him toward her. Long blond hair, streaked with light brown, framed the face of an angel. Not dainty, like she'd break any minute, but serene. Her eyes, the color of caramels, had a lovely depth to them. He'd never met another woman like her—then again, she wasn't of his time.

His time. The thought of it was still nuts.

"There's something about you . . . ," she started, then shook her head as if to banish an inappropriate thought. "I'm relieved that James is well. Are any of them hurt?"

She began walking back to her horse. Thank God he'd thought to tie them both up. And for his mother, who had taught all four of them to ride. At least now he understood her small quirks, which actually weren't quirks at all. Had she actually been preparing them for time travel? Or perhaps she'd just wanted them to learn things from her time out of nostalgia.

More importantly, how had he given Marian the impression that none of her men had been hurt?

Just say it, Greyson. Beating around the bush makes people think you're insincere.

Rhys had never needed their father's lessons. It was like he'd been born a carbon copy of the self-made man every New Orleanian admired. Not so him. But at least he'd listened.

He waited until they'd mounted, Greyson not sure if he would offend her by asking if she needed assistance. But she'd solved the problem by hiking up her gown and doing it more skillfully than him. Greyson supposed she rode more often than his once or so every year.

"I am sorry."

Clearly not fully recovered, she looked at him, her eyes too sorrowful for such a young woman. Was she even twenty-five?

Just say it.

"None of your men survived. If it's any consolation, none of the others did either."

She didn't believe him. One minute, she was looking up at him, shocked. Horrified. The next, she was riding ahead so fast Greyson could barely keep up. The clearing alongside the lake gave way to a thicket of woods. He hadn't survived his first battle just to break his neck falling from a damned horse.

"Hold up."

But she didn't hear him, or she didn't listen, so Greyson kept following her, doing his best not to make a total schmuck of himself. He made it to the road just as she launched herself from her horse, showing an enormous amount of agility despite her massive gown. She went straight to the body of the leader. Sir James, she'd called him.

Fenwall's marshal, according to Ross.

Of course, he had no idea who Fenwall was, but his uncle seemed to know just about everyone. An English earl, Ross had told him, and the woman who'd fled into the woods was his daughter.

As she threw herself atop the dead man, Greyson watched his uncle's men drag the bodies off the road.

"What will you do with them?" he asked one of the men, who threw him a suspicious look.

The men didn't know what to make of him. Ross had introduced him as a relative after warning him not to admit to being his nephew. They were much too close in age. Clearly the men didn't trust him yet, not that Greyson blamed them.

"We bury the Englishmen. The marauders can rot in hell."

When the guy's companion looked at him in shock, as if he'd said the worst sort of curse, Greyson took note. So apparently rotting in hell was the same as saying fuck in his time. Or maybe worse, judging by the second guy's expression.

The fact that they already had a couple of shovels with them had been an alarming discovery. So burying bodies was as par for the course as stopping to roast up some freshly caught rabbit?

Greyson didn't know if he should wash the blood from his hands, thankfully not his own, go to the woman, or help bury her friends. So he stood there for a moment, at a complete loss. Tough negotiations in the boardroom? Nothing compared to this.

He was out of his element. Big time.

And judging from the look on his uncle's face, it was only going to get worse.

7

THIS MORNING, Marian had little to recommend her.

Besides her horse, she had nothing but her gowns and the remainder of her dowry. The Scotsmen had saved that, at least, but it wasn't hers anyway—it belonged to the man she was supposed to marry, a man who cared as much for gold as he apparently did about a connection to the English king. Few were closer than her father to King Edward's inner circle, and though Marian was not privy to her betrothed's political leanings, she did know the Scotsman was keen to forge this alliance.

But material belongings mattered nothing to her. James was gone. Besides Gilda, he was the only person who'd ever shown her love. A good, kind man, he'd helped her navigate around her father.

One moment he'd been shouting for her to hide in the woods. The next, he was gone—his body as still as those she'd needed to step over to get to him.

They were all dead.

And if it weren't for the timely intervention of her new "friends," likely she would be dead too. Unless, as she'd overheard someone suggest, the reivers had targeted their group so they could kidnap or rob her. That possibility only made her feel worse.

Had this all been her fault?

Living so close to the border, she'd heard tales of the men who scourged the countryside, serving both northern and southern masters. Stealing, kidnapping, and murdering—taking advantage of the tumultuous and imaginary line between Scotsmen and Englishmen. But until now, it had never touched her life. Now, she felt unmoored. Lost.

"May I assist you, my lady?" asked the leader of the men.

Only then did she register they'd all stopped in front of an inn.

The leader of these men, despite his ever-present scowl, was as courtly as the most refined of Englishmen. He'd been attentive to her, assuring her she would find safe passage with them, though none knew where that passage should lead. Back to her father? To her betrothed? She'd be asked to make a decision soon.

That they had turned south after crossing the bridge had not fazed her. Marian could think of nothing except those bodies. And of James's still face, his eyes closed forever.

As the leader helped her down, Marian let herself glance around, trying to find *him*. Every so often he rode next to her. Once he'd asked her if she wished to speak about it. She'd shaken her head, and he had not spoken since. She often caught him watching her, though, and he'd likely seen her do the same. Sometimes Marian didn't even realize she had been staring until she caught herself and looked away.

There was just something strange about him. Something more than his unusual hairstyle or the way he spoke. More good-looking than most, but with a bearing that reinforced his claim of being a foreigner to this land . . . Marian stopped herself, feeling guilty for thinking in such a way after what had happened.

Despite herself, she glanced at the man leading her horse into the stables. Mayhap the foreigner was in there too? Marian was unsure of how long she stood there as the others scrambled around her.

"She's in shock."

Marian knew that voice already, despite having only heard it a few times. Deep and reverberating, it soothed her. She hadn't even seen him emerge. But darkness had fallen, the only light coming from above, the moon bright and full.

"Shock?"

That from a man named Alban, the long-haired warrior whose hauberk was still smeared with blood.

"Surprised," the foreigner clarified as Alban moved on. "Come inside with us."

She didn't move. Her men, all dead.

"We've not been properly introduced. Greyson McCaim, at your service."

At your service? What did that mean precisely?

"Never mind," he said with a shrug, "just my lame attempt to acclimate."

More unfamiliar words. "Do you speak Latin? Or French?"

She slipped into the latter but quickly realized he was unfamiliar with the language.

"Unfortunately, only English."

Finally gathering her wits as the others moved inside, the horses evidently stabled for the night, Marian remembered her manners.

"Lady Marian, daughter of the third Earl of Fenwall, if it pleases you."

He made a most ungentlemanly sound, something between a laugh and a snort, and then promptly apologized.

"Sorry. Lady Marian. Like in Robin Hood. Or was that Maid Marian?"

Cocking her head to the side, Marian attempted to make

sense of his words.

"Robin Hood?"

"It's a story. Evidently I'm too early though."

He was talking nonsense, but she found she did not want him to leave. At least he didn't expect her to speak of what had happened that day. She couldn't bear to do that. Not yet. "Will you tell me this story?"

"Greyson?" The leader waved for them to come into the inn. His tone rivaled that of her father, a man accustomed to being in command. She immediately began to comply.

But Greyson didn't move. "We'll be right there."

Marian stopped. "He is your leader."

"Yep. His name is Ross." He acknowledged Ross with a nod, and to her surprise, the big man followed the others inside, leaving them. The inn was a two-story wooden structure with light streaming from the open shutters. Up until now, she had rarely left Fenwall and stayed only twice at an inn, her father preferring the hospitality of others instead.

She should follow him inside. The last thing she should do was continue speaking to this perplexing, vexing, and very tempting man. And yet, she found herself asking him another question.

"Ross," she repeated. "He is from the mountains?"

Did she mean the Highlands? So much for Scottish nationalism. From what he'd gathered, the Lowlanders disliked the Highlanders almost as much as they disliked the English. The English disliked all Scots but the "mountain and island people" least of all. And his own family? Greyson wasn't even sure if they liked each other. They certainly had anger issues—ones that had likely saved Marian today.

"He's from the north." Kind of. Perthshire was at least north of Edinburgh, from what he remembered of his dad's maps. But he had a feeling Marian didn't really care about the answer. She hadn't spoken all day, and now wanted to talk about everything but what had happened. She was in need of a distraction. He'd felt that way often enough himself. He understood and would play along.

"Where I'm from, we have the same kind of divide. It's been years since the two sides fought, but sometimes there's still a lingering sense of being from the north. Or the south. We're different in a lot of ways."

She lifted an eyebrow. "And where, precisely, is that?"

He'd walked into that one, but he could only deflect.

"I will tell you. But only after you've eaten. Ross said he was getting rooms. Come inside."

Pulling up the hem of her gown, she followed him into the squat building.

He sucked in a breath as he stepped inside. Although he'd been in the past for two days now, it never failed to surprise him. It looked exactly like a scene from a movie.

Candles lit up the room from rough tables—planks of wood propped on top of barrels—and men feasted on huge bowls of what looked like oatmeal. The only woman besides Marian was a waitress, make that two of them. No bar or hostess stand.

Greyson chuckled to himself. What the hell else could he do? Had to keep a sense of humor or he'd go crazy.

"Have you not seen the inside of an inn before?" she asked curiously, taking note of his reaction.

Ross lifted his hand in greeting. They'd stopped along the way to wash in a freezing-cold river, but he'd give his right arm for a hot shower and one for Marian too.

Preferably, one for them to share.

"I have, of course. But I didn't see a village or anything nearby, so I guess I wasn't expecting much. This is . . ."

"The Bear and Bull. It's almost as well-known as The Wild Boar. Everyone crossing the border knows of it."

He stood in front of her, using his shoulders to cut a path to the others. It was like his favorite bar, The Dungeon, on a Saturday night. Only with more weapons. And no mixed drinks.

But Greyson didn't want to go down the rabbit hole of thinking about New Orleans and his life there, or what his brothers were doing back home. He was here, and that was a start. He'd find Rhys and their mother, no matter how long it took. Which was just as well because he had no idea if he could ever get back anyway.

At least he'd had the great luck to find Ross. After he'd proven himself to his uncle, Ross had simply said, "You are with me now."

Somehow, he'd found Greyson clothes that fit, a crossbow and quiver, and a horse. He had no idea how Ross had paid for them, nor could he hope to pay him back. Greyson didn't have a dime to his name. All he had was a phone that wouldn't have service for hundreds of years. The irony wasn't lost on him.

You are with me now.

He'd clung to those five words for the past two days to keep himself from going insane. Only the knowledge that he had help, that he wasn't alone, had kept him from obsessing over what had happened.

And then it occurred to him.

Turning just before they reached the table, he looked Lady Marian straight in the eyes. God, she was beautiful.

"You are with me now."

Hopefully that didn't have some hidden meaning, like they were suddenly married or something. But thankfully, she didn't look alarmed. Instead, his words had the effect he'd hoped they might. She actually smiled for the first time that day.

"Thank you," was all she said. But it was enough.

8

MARIAN CUPPED the fast-running water into her hands and drank from it. She hadn't expected much time to herself, but the sound of a cracking branch behind her meant her solace was at an end. A quick glance told her that her visitor was Greyson, however, and her reluctance shifted to eagerness.

When he was near, she felt better. Her preoccupation with trying to understand him kept her mind from the events of yesterday. From the sight that had greeted her on the road and the realization that she had narrowly missed the same fate, or worse.

"You never did tell me where you're from," she reminded him. Greyson crossed his arms and leaned against a tree just next to her. "Nor did you tell me the tale you promised."

"Tale?"

She stood, shaking her hands to dry them.

"Of Robin Hood? And Maid Marian?"

Though he appeared relaxed from a distance, the pretense slipped away as he came closer. A tic in his jaw, something she'd noticed before, was on display.

He was as troubled as she.

"Does something have you worried?" she asked before think-ing. "I apologize, 'twas impolite to ask such a thing."

He appeared genuinely confused. "Impolite? I do not consider it so."

Suddenly, she remembered something. "Yesterday in the woods, when you called to me. You used my given name."

She distinctly remembered him calling *Marian* rather than *Lady Marian*. But that was not the only occasion he'd shunned formality. "You are more . . . familiar than I am accustomed."

"You don't typically hug strangers?"

"Nay, I do not." Which is when she realized he'd said it in jest.

"Lady Marian"—he emphasized her title—"when I searched for you, I worried for your safety."

"And I thank you for your concern." He didn't appear inclined to offer further explanation. "The men are ready?"

"Almost. Ross wants to talk to you."

Her shoulders sagged. Marian knew what he would ask her, and she had no answer for him.

Something about her expression must have roused Greyson's curiosity, for he cocked his head, studying her, and asked, "Do we take you back to Fenwall? Or will you continue with us to Quinting Castle and then Pittillock when we return?"

Not for the first time Marian wondered what business these Scotsmen had at Quinting. She'd heard them talking at supper, something about speaking with Edward's regent, but she knew precious little else. Of course, she had not been very forth-coming either, saying only that they'd been headed to Pittillock before the attack. If she told them, there was a risk they might leave with the remainder of her dowry, which was being carried on a packhorse, treated as no different than her chest of gowns.

And yet, she found herself wanting to tell Greyson. She wanted to trust him, and although her father would call her foolish, she trusted the impulse.

"My betrothed waits for me in Pittillock."

She did not miss his look of disappointment. If only this man knew how very much she wished to be free from the arrangement.

"If I return to my father, he will be wroth with me for breaking our agreement."

Greyson shifted his weight against the tall oak.

"He'll be mad at you for being attacked?"

She did not hesitate. "Aye. I was to be married by midmonth. So you see, either way I will not be at Pittillock as per my father's arrangement with the Earl of Fife."

Greyson scowled, his eyes flashing.

"Are you kidding me? You were attacked, for God's sakes. How is that your fault?"

He did speak so strangely, but she found she quite liked his bluntness. Too few people spoke their minds openly.

"It is my understanding the Earl of Fife is neither a kind nor understanding man. Very much like the son, Duncan, who I am to marry. The reason will matter naught. They will demand a higher dowry, which my father will gladly pay to bring about this union. But he will be angered either way."

With every word she said, Greyson looked angrier, his hands clenched into fists, his mouth as flat as a blade. Although she was grateful he was upset on her behalf, she didn't understand it. These matters were hardly unusual. She'd even heard tales of women being kidnapped to delay or alter a marriage agreement.

"You haven't met him?"

Marian attempted to smooth out the front of her gown. Without proper lying time, it was wrinkled beyond repair. Silly that she should care about such a thing, but it made her feel better, presenting herself well.

"Nay. I have not."

"Do you want to marry him?"

What a funny question.

"Again, that familiarity," she said with a small smile. "As if we've known each other forever." She wished she could tell him how much she liked it, but that would never do. Whether she wanted to marry the man or not, she had no choice. Her father's will was the only one that mattered.

He reached her in three strides. "Do you want to marry him?" he pressed.

Marian's breath caught at his tone. "I . . ." How could she answer such a question? "It is my duty to forge this alliance."

"What will happen if you go back to Fenwall?"

Marian imagined the reception she would receive. "Father will yell, of course." She smiled. "But I would be sure to stand well away from his spittle."

"How can you joke?" He cut off whatever he'd been about to say, shaking his head. "And his men? What will he say of his men?"

She'd wondered about that as well. "He will likely attempt to learn more about the attack."

He stood much too close, his eyes holding hers, beseeching her to continue.

"The remainder of my dowry is in that second trunk we carry. 'Twas possible the reivers who attacked us knew of its value and planned to rob us. Or mayhap they thought to kidnap me. Father will want to know if it was planned."

"But the reivers are all dead."

Marian shrugged, attempting to appear casual despite his closeness.

"Certainly, there are more of them. Their families still live. The reivers' strength is in their bonds to each other and their knowledge of the terrain."

"Family," he muttered. And it was there again, that sadness she'd glimpsed in him every so often. When he'd told her the news about James, about her men, she'd seen grief in his eyes. He understood, because he'd lost people too.

"Stay with us."

Marian blinked.

"Stay with us. Come to Quinting. And then we'll take you to Pittillock."

In truth, it was the same conclusion she'd reached. If she went home, her father would merely send her back. She might as well continue. Besides which, she'd be with Greyson. Although it could not lead anywhere, she wished to spend as much time with him as she could.

"Very well."

The glint of surprise in his eyes told her she'd not negotiated very well. He hadn't expected her immediate agreement. So Marian quickly added, "If you will tell me where you come from."

More surprise, and then the corners of his mouth lifted to reveal straight white teeth and a most wicked grin. "You drive a hard bargain, Lady Marian."

"Marian," she blurted before thinking. "You may call me Marian."

"I get the feeling I should be honored."

He did not say it sarcastically, but as if he were genuinely curious, and so she gave him a serious answer. "None but my father calls me such." She paused, then added, "Not even my maid who raised me like a mother."

He looked shocked, mayhap even humbled. "But you offer it to me?"

"Aye, so you may choose to be honored, if it pleases you. But I hope it will also please you to tell me, where are you from that strangers address each other as relatives?"

He didn't answer at first. That tic in his jaw was back, and she could tell he was considering her request.

"Do not run," he finally said. "Or scream. Or think I'm completely crazy."

"Crazy?"

"Never mind. Please just listen to me. I'm going to tell you something I shouldn't. But I want you to know you can trust me."

She thought of the way he'd called for her in that wood, his voice frantic as he spoke her given name.

"I already do."

Marian could actually hear him breathing. She waited, wondering. Curious now . . .

"I am from . . ." Greyson swallowed, appearing nervous for the first time since they'd met. "I am from the future."

9

———

Yeah, he probably shouldn't have led with that.

Go with your gut.

So much of what he'd learned about business, and life, had come from his father and even Rhys, but that particular tenet had been his mother's. Before she'd disappeared, leaving behind the misconception that she'd purposefully abandoned their family, Greyson had thought his mother could do no wrong. Although he was relieved to know he'd been right about her, that she hadn't left them, he really shouldn't have pulled up that piece of advice just now. Because judging from the look on Maid Marian's face, she wasn't having it.

She most definitely thought him *mad*, as they would say in this time.

"Please don't run."

Greyson grabbed her wrist, aware their names were being called in the clearing. He'd come down to get her, not spill the beans on his very sordid tale. His uncle would be furious if he found out. But Greyson wanted to know Marian, and for her to know him, and it had felt natural to tell her.

"We have to go back soon, but please just listen to me. It

sounds bonkers. I know. But my aunt, Ross's sister, knows spells."

"Ross MacKinnish is your uncle?"

Greyson had to give her credit. Although she still looked dubious, she hadn't attempted to pull away. The hand on her wrist was unnecessary, although he kept it there because he liked the feel of it. She actually seemed intrigued. Not scared.

"He is. And my mother and brother are here too. My mother is from here, from Castle Hightower in Perthshire, and somehow her sister sent her through time, to the future. But she was pulled back five years ago. We thought she'd left us. But then my father got sick and . . ." He grabbed the back of his neck, letting her go. "And we went through his study. Apparently he hadn't gone craz—mad, after all. He'd been right all along. There was this spell"—aware he was losing her, he spoke more quickly—"and a book, with some missing information, I guess. But my brother, Rhys, he knows Gaelic. I don't know what he did to solve the puzzle, but . . ."

Marian's eyes narrowed as she took a step away from him, shaking her wrist free. Of course she didn't believe him. He hadn't believed his own father, after all.

Pulling out his phone, which couldn't have much of a charge left, Greyson pressed the button to turn it on. When the screen lit up, Marian looked absolutely terrified. And no wonder—it had to look like witchcraft. But it was the only way he could convince her to listen.

"What . . . what is that?"

He really shouldn't have told her.

"A cell phone. You can use it to talk to people from far away. And look, these are pictures. Like drawings but . . . watch."

He stepped back, snapped a picture, and then held the phone out to her.

"See? It's you."

Her eyes went huge.

The calls became shouts. "We really have to go." Greyson turned the phone off. "I'm aware that I sound like a raving lunatic, but I can assure you I'm not. I co-own a shipping company with my brothers. We're actually . . ."

Billionaires. Well respected in the community, or at least they had been. If the reporters had been descending on the mansion before he'd left, surely they'd be even more eager for a story now. For all he knew, all of the McCaim siblings could have disappeared. Reikart or Ian could even be here by now. They'd promised that anyone left behind would keep trying to join the others.

But none of that mattered to this beautiful woman whose father would blame her for being attacked. Who'd been betrothed to a cruel man she'd never even met.

To her, he was a complete and utter loon.

"Marian . . ." Using a woman's first name had never seemed so intimate before. "Please believe that I am of sound mind and body. It sounds crazy, but I am telling the truth. I've been in your century for exactly two days. And trust me, it's been more of an adjustment than a New Orleans boy learning how to deal with snow."

He started walking and, thankfully, she fell in step beside him.

"My century?"

Greyson supposed he should be happy. Marian was humoring him. Although she clearly didn't believe him, she didn't appear to be freaked out enough to go running for the hills. It was a start. "I'm from the twenty-first century."

She actually giggled. A delightful, fun sound that immediately lifted his mood. When they got back to the others, Ross scowled at him—*I gave you one job*—but not even his Viking uncle's wrath could dampen his mood.

"You did ask," Greyson said to her in an undertone. Aware

they were within earshot of the others now, he refrained from saying much more.

"Aye," she agreed. "I suppose I did. Tell me more of this phone."

Though she didn't quite believe him, Marian also was having difficulty reconciling his cell with her world. Which was exactly what he'd hoped for.

"Most people have them. You can speak to people around the world. Look up facts and take pictures. I didn't think I could live without it." But obviously he was doing just that.

"Lady Marian, a word, if you please?" Ross said, his voice a deep rumble.

He accompanied her to his uncle, who was tightening a leather strap on his horse's saddle.

"Have you made a decision regarding your destination? If we are to go to Fenwall—"

"I will accompany you to Quinting Castle if you should be kind enough to escort me to Pittillock once your business in England is complete."

Ross looked back and forth between them. "And your father?"

"I will send a missive to him from Quinting. And to my betrothed as well."

Greyson didn't flinch. He watched his uncle closely, realizing he'd already known about her circumstances. Ross had intuited she'd been traveling north to be married.

"You will, of course, be paid handsomely for your efforts."

Ross glanced over to the packhorse then. Specifically, to one of Marian's two trunks.

"Keep the rest of your dowry. No payment is needed. Your man . . ."

"Sir James. Fenwall's marshal."

Ross nodded. "Sir James provided us with much-needed

information on the current state of Quinting Castle and its guests. We repay his kindness by offering you safe passage."

"It seems you've repaid his kindness already by keeping me alive." She looked at him then.

But Greyson hadn't played the part of a hero. Not really. He'd never admit it, especially not to his brothers, if he ever saw them again, but the battle had terrified him. It was nothing like the movies. The sound of metal clashing against metal, accompanied by men's shouts of pain, of *death*—it was something he never wanted to hear again. The violence of it had made the epic bar fight that had earned Ian a night in jail look like a children's Saturday-morning cartoon by comparison.

If his bow hadn't been already readied, he would have been completely useless. As it was, Greyson had needed to dismount before he took the first shot. Mounted archery had never really been his thing.

No, he would not take credit for something the other men had done. "You can thank Clan MacKinnish for that." He nodded toward Ross. "They did not hesitate."

Marian curtsied as if she'd been doing it her entire life. Which, of course, she had.

"'Tis settled, then." With that, Marian strode to her horse as calmly as if she hadn't just seen a cell phone and been informed one of her travel partners was from the future.

Who is this woman?

Watching her walk away, Greyson found himself thinking of his ex-girlfriend. They looked nothing alike, Marian as blonde and refined as Lisa was dark and brash. Their personalities were night and day too. The drama with his father's strange illness, which apparently hadn't been an illness after all, had driven Lisa off. She'd said it made things too real. He suspected Marian would have been able to handle that, and much, much more. This woman could handle just about anything, it seemed.

Realizing Ross was looking at him, Greyson cleared his throat.

"How did you know she was engaged?"

In response, his uncle crossed his arms as he tended to do when he was unhappy with something Greyson had said. It happened a lot.

"Betrothed," he corrected, belatedly remembering his uncle's warning about standing out. He'd blown that one, all right.

"There are very few reasons why an earl's daughter would venture across the border with so many men and two trunks, one of which is too heavy to contain anything other than gold."

It seemed he had a lot to learn.

Not wanting to talk about Marian, specifically about her *betrothed* . . . oh, and the fact that he'd revealed his secret to her, Greyson changed the subject.

"Do you really think we'll learn anything about Shona at . . ." What was the name of it? "Quinting Castle?"

At least he'd remembered not to call her Mom. Greyson smiled, maybe a bit too smugly for Ross's liking. Admittedly, it wasn't a stunning success.

"If Irvine's as well-placed as Grace says, then he's wealthy enough to be known to the kind of people who frequent the king's Northumbrian court. It's taken some time to find him, but some place him currently at Quinting, a popular destination for hunting this time of year."

Greyson had no choice but to pretend he understood half of what his uncle had just said. Before he could respond, Ross yelled, "Ride out." Without another word, he stalked to his horse, pulling himself up as easily as if he weren't six-foot-something and two-hundred-plus pounds. The Saints' defense could use someone like him. Although Ross would just as soon cut his way through the opposing team as he would tackle them.

The man was an animal.

A memory from the battle was burned into his brain—his

uncle standing with that giant sword raised high overhead. Greyson had watched in mingled awe and horror as he brought that sword down on one of the reivers. By then Greyson had let more than half of the arrows he carried fly. Miraculously, he'd managed to fell a man. He'd never doubted his ability to aim and shoot. But with a crossbow like the one slung across his saddle? And in the middle of the bloodiest fight he'd ever witnessed?

His archery coach would be proud.

Hell, his mother would be proud. She'd loved coming to his matches. Didn't matter where it was, his mother, if not both of his parents, would fly in to his match, take him and his friend to dinner, and fly back to New Orleans.

One of the benefits of having *more money than God*, as Ian would say.

Money that hadn't done shit for them in the end. His mom had still gone missing. His dad had fallen into a coma. Now his mother and his brother were both somewhere in medieval Scotland, and looking for them without the internet or any modern technology felt a whole lot like sifting through hay for a needle.

Although he'd wanted his brothers to join him—he'd thought it best for them to stay together—the past days had changed his mind. Life here was brutal, and one or both of them could die if they followed him.

Stay there. Please, stay.

He repeated it over and over again in his mind as he mounted his horse. Of course, he knew Reikart and Ian couldn't hear him. They were probably saying that damn chant even now, still trying to get it right.

With any luck, and his family didn't seem to have much of it, they wouldn't figure it out. They would stay safe in New Orleans, look after their father and the business. And live.

Without knowing where all of us are. If we're dead or alive.

It was no way to live, and Greyson knew it. Every day for the past five years he'd tried, unsuccessfully, to move on. To forget that their mother had left them. To push away the niggling doubt that his father might not be crazy after all, that his mother was really in trouble.

It hadn't worked for him, and it sure as hell wouldn't work for his brothers.

Pretty much, they were all good and fucked.

10

"Holy shit."

Greyson had been to Scotland before, with his family. But he'd missed out on seeing Edinburgh Castle. On the day the rest of them had gone, he'd been back in the hotel vomiting. To this day he thought it was probably food poisoning. But his mother, who'd stayed back to take care of him, had disagreed.

Food poisoning, a stomach virus. Whatever it was, it had disappeared almost as quickly as it had come on. That was the only tour they'd missed. But Greyson couldn't imagine the castle everyone had come back raving about was any more impressive than this one.

Nearly two full days after he'd screwed up, telling Marian the very thing he should have kept secret, they rode over a ridge that gave them a full view of the *court in the north*, as Ross had called it.

"There are no castles where you are from?"

She rode up next to him, teasing as always. He suspected it was her natural state, although the reality of her situation caught up with her at times, and when it did, she looked very much as if her world had ended. Friends taken, and pretty violently too. A betrothed who Greyson hated more and more every time she talked about him. Which wasn't much except when he asked questions. He knew the important parts. Marian's father, who also seemed like a bit of a dick, wanted an alliance with the Scottish Earl of Fife, and that was pretty much the beginning and the end of her story, in terms of her impending nuptials.

But he'd learned a few other things about her, namely, she wasn't as uptight as he'd expect from an English earl's daughter. In fact, just the opposite. Marian laughed easily, joked with the men as if she'd known them her whole life. Self-deprecating, she talked about how easily she forgot information. When Alban had asked when she'd acquired such a poor memory, Marian had thought about it for a few moments and said, "I forget."

The big, hulking Vikings they were traveling with had laughed at that—big, deep belly laughs—and Greyson had almost forgotten, if only briefly, that he was living in a dream, or near enough. It was like that around Marian. She woke him up.

If only he hadn't opened his mouth about the whole time travel thing. Greyson almost wished it had freaked her out. Instead, she treated it as a big joke. At every turn, Marian whispered things like, "There are no castles where you're from?" not even pretending to be serious.

Still, it was better than her spilling the beans to the others.

After realizing his efforts to convince her of the truth weren't working, Greyson had started playing along. His phone clearly hadn't done the trick, and now the battery was dead. Although Marian still asked about it, she seemed to think it some kind of clever trick rather than proof of his story.

"Nay," he teased back, the term flowing more easily from his tongue, "there are not. And definitely not like that one."

"There are few to rival it along the borderlands. At least here in England. Kenshire, perhaps."

This was the second time he'd heard they had passed the border. He wasn't sure when the hell that had happened, but apparently England looked exactly like its northern neighbor.

"Are they very different, England and Scotland? They look much the same. People seem to dress the same. I'll admit my history is lacking in this area." None were close enough to hear them, but even so, he shouldn't have made such a slip. It would be too easy to do it around the wrong person.

"Your history." The corners of Marian's very full lips turned up. "If you were more learned in this area, you would know borderers' first loyalty lies with themselves. And other borderers. Then perhaps to their own countrymen."

"And women."

They rode at the back of the pack, but Greyson could see guards moving at the top of the castle walls. They were everywhere. What a different sight than pulling into a parking lot on the castle grounds and seeing a line for tours.

This was the real deal.

When Marian didn't respond, he glanced over to find her puzzled.

"And women?" she asked, her brow creased.

It struck him then that his mother must have loved the future.

"In my time, we'd say both—countrymen *and* women. Although to be fair, I don't recall hearing a lot of people say 'countrywomen,' but my mother would have. She was pretty careful about using inclusive language, and I suspect I know why."

"Inclusive language?"

Jesus. They might as well be talking two different languages.

"When you say man, what does it make you think of?"

"Someone such as you?" She offered the question innocently, so Greyson knew he should take it that way. Though the idea of being a model of manhood for this woman was much too appealing.

"But not a woman, right?"

Marian shook her head. "Certainly not."

"And that's the point. Language has power. Words matter. Inclusive language means, in this case, including both men and women."

In that moment, watching Marian blink as she attempted to grasp the concept of women being included in anything, Greyson realized his mother had been this woman once. Raised in thirteenth-century Scotland. What a shock it must have been to her to find herself in the future, in New Orleans, no less . . .

He'd always admired his mother, but no more so than now. She'd overcome so much to become the strong, warm, brilliant woman who'd raised him. Marian deserved the chance to be her own woman too, but she wouldn't get it. After Ross delivered the Guardian's message, they would escort Marian to her fiancé. Shit. Greyson shifted in the rudimentary saddle, troubled by the thought of leaving her with a man like Duncan.

But how could he avoid it?

They stopped just before the drawbridge, which was actually down. What was the point of a moat and drawbridge if it wasn't raised? Everywhere he looked, there were fully armored knights. A small army of them.

"Are all castles this heavily guarded?"

Marian looked at him as if it were the strangest question he'd ever asked. What had he done wrong now? It was almost like being back home under his CEO brother's watchful gaze. Rhys had always looked at him like that, questioning and a little disapproving, when he didn't agree with him.

"When the king's regent is in attendance, yes."

Made sense.

"Edmund of Cornwall," she said as they waited for Ross to get them into the castle.

"Pardon?"

"The second Earl of Cornwall. The king's lieutenant on his campaign in Wales, now his regent since King Edward has left for Gascony. The earl was born in Hertfordshire but resides in Quinting Castle during the summer months. He will very likely return south soon."

"I see."

Marian brought her mount closer to him and spoke more softly. "You realize, do you not, that your uncle"—she said the word as if she still didn't believe their relationship—"is an important man?"

Must run in the family.

"I know he's bringing a message from the Guardians of Scotland, a bunch of guys who decided to accept a baby as their heir. That's what he's supposed to be telling your regent."

Greyson decided this proper Englishwoman rolling her eyes at him was much preferable to Ian doing it.

"Those 'guys,' as you call them, are the most important men in your kingless country at the moment."

"Yeah, Ross said the man he serves is pretty important. And history seems to agree."

"Robert the Bruce?"

"Yep."

"I would imagine there's a reason he and men like Balliol and Comyn were not appointed as Guardians."

He didn't know who they were, but the history lesson would have to wait. They were moving again, and as they passed his uncle, he sensed the man's mood had changed. He definitely wasn't happy.

"Something wrong?"

Ross darted a glance at Marian. "Nay," he said, his thick brogue sounding even thicker, as if he'd become more Scottish as they traveled deeper into England. "The opposite. *He* is here."

Greyson was as confused as Marian for a second, thinking

he meant the regent. Of course the regent was here—wasn't that the whole point?

"Oh," Greyson said, realizing who his uncle meant. Irvine. "Good."

He gave Marian a look that promised an explanation later. But right now, shit was about to hit the fan. At least one of the people responsible for his mother's disappearance into the future was in this castle. And based on what he'd witnessed two days ago, they dealt with attempted murder a bit differently in this time.

Things were about to get really interesting.

11

MARIAN HAD NEVER RELISHED a bath quite so much as this one. It felt wonderful to wash off the long days on the road, the horrible attack. Her father may have been absent, at best, but he had always kept her sheltered at Fenwall. Lonely, but pampered. Purposeless, but well treated.

When she'd first left for Pittillock, a small part of her had craved the adventure she had always sought. A very, very small part. She'd never have chosen to marry Duncan, of course, but it had at least been an opportunity to venture into the world. The prospect had soured further when Gilda had been ordered to stay home, but a spark of hope had remained in Marian's chest. Adventure had found her, after all, but at a horrible cost.

A quick knock was followed by the appearance of the same lady's maid who had overseen the filling of the tub. Marian stepped out of the water, blushing as she covered herself with a drying cloth. She chided herself for the show of modesty. For someone of her rank, it was both normal and expected to be attended by servants. But Marian rarely traveled, and her maid had practically raised her from a babe.

"Your gown is laid out, my lady," said the girl. "Shall I help prepare you for supper?"

"I would thank you to do so."

As Marian dropped the drying cloth and stepped into her hose, the girl moved so deftly Marian had no doubt she'd been serving here for years despite her young age. Ten and six, perhaps?

"I've not been to Quinting Castle before," she said, impressed at both its size and opulence. "Inside the great hall, one could hardly tell the sun had set."

Another of the maids had offered her a tour, which she'd gladly accepted. The men were off seeing to their business, and it was the first time in her life she could ever remember having no one to answer to at all. The freedom was thrilling. Roaming the estate, Marian had been struck by the candles and torches that filled every room, keeping it bright despite the growing dusk. Her father was wealthy, but he abhorred waste, and they'd never been allowed to use more than the necessary number of candles and torches.

"Visitors sometimes say they can spy the keep from the other side of the Torshire River."

Marian did not doubt it.

"The men who arrived with us . . ." Marian ducked for the girl to help her slip on the deep green kirtle. "Have you seen them recently, by chance?"

"I have not, my lady."

Sitting on the edge of the bed, Marian closed her eyes as the girl ran an ivory comb through her hair. "Do I smell thyme?"

"Aye, my lady. And mint."

She was accustomed to Gilda's perfumes. This one was unfamiliar, but sweeter for it.

The maid started to pull her hair away from her face, but she requested to wear it down, something she always did at home.

"Surely I should use some adornment?" the girl asked.

Though many years her junior, the young maid sounded very much like Gilda in this. But as always, Marian refused.

"You may leave it loose."

Though she would be expected to wear it up once she was married, she was still a free woman. And this was one thing she could control.

"I will be covering it soon enough."

The girl didn't comment but finished her ministrations. Standing back, she seemed pleased. "You look lovely, my lady."

"Many thanks for your assistance."

Just before leaving the chamber, the girl called back, "A chambermaid will be along shortly to remove the tub, and I shall find an escort for you to supper."

The practice was customary in a great household such as this one, but Marian contemplated making her own way to the great hall. She'd enjoyed her taste of freedom, and surely she could find it easily enough. A knock on the door interrupted her thoughts. Marian waited for the chambermaid, or her escort, to enter. Instead, another knock landed on the wood.

She opened it and sucked in her breath. Freshly washed, he'd somehow acquired a black surcoat trimmed in royal blue and gold. He appeared a true nobleman, but with an edge none of the men here could possibly hope to match. Marian had purposely not allowed her thoughts to stray to this very man. They'd been too consumed with him of late, and Marian was unsure what to believe. His claim was simply so fantastical. She'd gone out of her way to convince him she did not believe it. And she truly didn't . . .

Except she couldn't banish the memory of that image, the one in the little black box, or ignore the fact that he simply didn't belong here. He didn't know any of the things he ought to know or talk like he should talk . . .

"I sent away your escort. Hope that's okay?"

Okay? Aye, there was no doubt he spoke like no one she'd ever heard before.

"You know the keep well, do you?" She stepped back and swept her hand inside, indicating he should enter. Reaching behind him, Marian closed the door as their eyes locked. Quickly turning back to the chamber, Marian began to blow out the candles that had been lit for her. Chambermaids would continue to stoke the fireplace, but keeping candles lit in an unattended room was akin to wishing for disaster. Thankfully, she'd been able to avoid starting a fire herself despite her occasional clumsiness.

When she finished, the only light from the chamber coming from the fireplace, Marian joined Greyson. She'd been alone in a bedchamber with a man before, of course. But they had been servants. And this felt very, very different.

"As well as any keep. It's only the fourth one I've been inside in my life, and the other three were on tours."

Marian found she enjoyed teasing him on the topic, even though it truly wasn't funny. She should think him mad, but he didn't seem mad. Nor could she forget the things he'd shown her, told her.

"In what type of dwelling, pray tell, do you live in . . ."

"New Orleans. In America. The United States of America."

She would play along simply because she wanted to stay here with him. To talk with him. Once they left her chamber, Greyson's clan would demand his attention.

"New Orleans," she repeated. "Tell me about this place."

Greyson made a sound that reminded her, once again, that they should probably leave. It was much too tempting to be this close to him, to be alone with him, but she wasn't ready to step away from him just yet.

"New Orleans is the best city in the world. It has its problems, like any city, but the mix of cultures, the music, the food . . . there's nowhere quite like it. When I left for college"—he smiled—"university, I liked traveling in the Northeast. There are some great places up there too. Boston, especially. But New Orleans is in my blood. I'll never leave it. Unless coastal erosion forces my hand."

She was about to ask what he meant by "coastal erosion" when Greyson shook his head. "So much you don't know about. Thinking of Boston reminds me of a really interesting story involving your people and mine."

"Clan MacKinnish?"

"No, the Americans. And the English."

"I do not know this . . . America."

"You wouldn't." He shifted his weight between his feet, as if he wanted to leave. As if he felt uncomfortable being alone with her. It was the only thing that could have convinced her to go. Stepping past him, Marian attempted to do just that when his hand on her arm stopped her. Though she couldn't feel him through the heavy fabric of her gown, Marian had a very clear memory of being held in this man's arms. She thought about it each night.

"I think you misunderstand."

They stood so close now, Marian could feel the vibrations of his deep voice. She knew she should step away but could not.

"We should be moving along," she said, her voice tight.

"Marian."

She looked up, and wished she hadn't. That look . . . it was much too *knowing*.

"I don't know how it is in your time."

My time. As if he truly means it. But he did, of course he did. She knew that. She'd known it all along. The question was whether she could suspend her own disbelief to believe it too.

"But in mine, when a woman is engag—betrothed, that means hands off."

Her heart beat faster in her chest. Was he implying . . . ?

"Otherwise, I'd have kissed you ten times over. Or more,

maybe. But I have a feeling that's frowned upon now. If the history I know is true."

He dropped his hand, and a good thing because Marian could not back away quick enough. The thought of him kissing her . . . she'd been kissed once, and though the experience had been pleasant, she had a feeling it would be even more so with him.

It would make it that much harder to do what she needed to do and marry her intended.

"'Tis not proper in my time"—she couldn't help a small smile at that—"for an unwed woman to be alone with a man this way. Unless, of course, he is a servant."

"Of course."

"Nor is the discussion of such topics considered appropriate."

"Hmmm." Greyson took a step toward her, standing so close she could smell the river on him. So he'd bathed in the nearby river. A chilly prospect, to be sure. The thought of his bare chest dripping with water made her bite her bottom lip.

"In my time"—she stared at his lips as he spoke—"a woman chooses her own husband."

"Oh. Some do here, of course, as well."

"I mean nearly all of them do," he corrected, "even the wealthy ones."

Her brows furrowed. "How do you make alliances, then?"

"I'd be happy to tell you about social circles and the antics of the rich and famous, but suffice it to say, people think of alliances very differently in the twenty-first century."

"Rich and famous . . ." She could hardly think with him so close, his breath warm on her cheek. "Are you rich and famous?"

"Yes."

His answer was so quick to come Marian had no doubt it was true.

"My father owns, owned, a shipping company based in the

Port of New Orleans. My brothers and I took it over a few years ago."

"You have brothers?"

"I do. Three of them. One came through time before I did, which is how I knew my father was right about my mother's disappearance. We really did think the grief of losing her had driven him mad."

Marian wasn't sure what to say.

"Long story short, my father became ill, went into a coma . . . a deep sleep. But before he did, Dad begged us to come find mom. We figured we owed him at least a look around his study, which he always kept locked. Even my youngest brother, Ian, who lives with him, hasn't been allowed in that study in years. Which is strange since Dad wanted us to believe him. Maybe he was afraid we'd take the things he'd collected. None of us wanted to encourage his flights of fancy."

Despite herself, she had to ask. "What happened to your brother, the one who you said came through time?"

"Rhys? He was the one who figured it out somehow. We'd found the chant, the one my aunt apparently used with my mother. But there was also an ancient book of spells in the study, something my dad had bought at an auction. Rhys tore into it, started muttering something about the wrong words, and then wrote down a different version of the chant. We thought it was bullshit, to be honest. But we grabbed the old cross like my father's notes said to do, recited Rhys's new and improved chant, and . . . yeah . . ."

Greyson winced.

"He disappeared."

"Disappeared?" she repeated.

"Quicker than my brother Ian used to take off whenever my mother gave us chores. Gone."

Aware they stood much too close, Marian backed away just enough to see his face without straining her neck. If only they could remain here all eve rather than attending supper in the hall. She was about to ask what had happened next when another knock on the door was followed by the appearance of two young male servants. Their eyes widened at the sight of them.

"Apologies my lady, my lord. We expected you to be gone already to supper."

The wooden buckets they carried announced they were here to empty the tub, an undertaking that would take some time.

"No apologies necessary. We were leaving for supper now. Thank you for the bath."

Both boys bowed their heads as Marian hurried from the chamber, Greyson following her into the corridor. She stopped suddenly.

"When we arrived, Ross said, 'He's here,' and I'll admit I've been wondering about that all day. Is all well? Who is 'he'?"

Greyson's fists clenched.

"*He* is a man by the name of Yearger Irvine."

Marian did not know of him.

"And he is here at Quinting Castle? Do you not care for this man?"

Greyson made a sound that very clearly indicated his answer. "Care for a man who tried to kill my mother? Not so much."

"Tried to kill your mother?" she asked in an undertone, looking about to ensure no one had overheard them. They were alone in the passageway. "This man is here? What are you planning?"

If so, Marian had a feeling his days left on this earth were few in number. Although Greyson was quick with a jest, he looked serious and deadly now, in the bright torchlight.

"Was here. We're told he's gone on some overnight hunting trip and is expected back tomorrow." Greyson bent his elbow, and Marian slipped her arm inside. "My only real plan is to follow my uncle's lead. But Yearger Irvine is the real reason he volunteered to take the Guardians of Scotland's message here in the first place."

"And what do you suppose your uncle is planning?" she asked, belatedly realizing she'd fallen into step with Greyson's claim of Ross being his uncle. But the shape of their faces, their strong, distinctive jawlines, was eerily similar.

"He hasn't said exactly, but I hope this Yearger is enjoying his hunting trip. I'm pretty sure it will be his last one."

Marian glanced over to confirm Greyson was quite serious.

"So how exactly do y'all deal with murder in the Middle Ages?"

12

CHRIST, she was beautiful.

Greyson sat across from her at a table that looked like some kind of portable picnic table. But much nicer. Unlike him, Marian fit into this world perfectly. When she'd opened her bedroom door earlier, Greyson had forgotten about everything for a moment. His dad lying in a hospital bed, in a coma. His mother and brother running around Scotland somewhere . . . or dead. Reikart and Ian . . . who in the hell knew where, or *when*, they were?

Greyson had to remind himself this trip to Quinting Castle wasn't a delay. They'd come here to find one of the men responsible for his mother's disappearance. Responsible for trying to kill her, according to Ross.

He found himself thinking again about fate, and how it had brought him and Ross together. Had it brought him to Marian too? Perhaps they had been meant to help her. To stop those men from murdering her like they had her companions.

Nonsense. He was taking the idea way too far.

"So how did my lady come to be in the company of these men?"

Asshole.

Unfortunately, they were seated with two men outside of their party—"Englishmen," Ross had muttered like a curse when they were seated. He hadn't bothered to whisper, which was probably the reason they seemed so pissed off now. Between the two of them, Greyson was pretty sure every color in the rainbow was represented.

"When my father's men were murdered by a group of border reivers, these men saved my life," Marian said. "And ensured our attackers met with the justice they deserved."

She said it so prettily, Greyson could hardly believe she'd just told the English dandies her father's men had been slaughtered. Her bluntness did its job. The guy was clearly at a loss for words, although that didn't stop him from eyeing Marian like she was the next course. If he didn't look away soon, Greyson would find out how they handled rudeness in the thirteen century. Because in his time, this guy would already have a black eye.

But it wasn't the time or the place for a brawl. They sat in a hall filled with more than a hundred other men and women, surrounded by at least double that in candles, and the head table looked like it was literally made of gold, or at least gilded with it . . .

Greyson wasn't the only one on his best behavior. His uncle had admitted that Yearger's temporary absence may have been a blessing. He couldn't guarantee what would happen when they questioned him, so perhaps it was best done away from the castle. This way he could at least deliver the Guardians' message in the spirit of diplomacy in which it had been intended.

Their personal mission could come later.

"We should be thankful for your assistance, then," the dandy finally said to Ross, who was clearly their leader.

Music began to play in the corner of the hall. Greyson couldn't see the musicians, but the sound was as fine as any of the symphonies he'd attended. If only his mother could see such an affair. She had always loved throwing elaborate dinner parties . . .

She *had* seen such a thing before. Jesus! According to Ross, his mother had been a lady-in-waiting to the Queen of Scotland. A few appetizers and drinks for the New Orleans elite must have been child's play for her.

His uncle grunted. "English reivers, by the look of them," he shot back. His attachment to diplomacy was apparently only so strong.

"Hmm. Seems odd, indeed, for English reivers to attack the daughter of the Earl of Fenwall."

Unless they knew about the dowry. But he kept that thought to himself. Ross had ordered him to speak as little as possible. Besides, it probably wasn't the best idea to advertise the fact that she carried a trunk of gold, even in this audience.

After he figured out what to do with the piece of bread that had been placed in front of him—apparently it was actually a plate—Greyson resigned himself to the role of observer for the evening. He listened to the exchanges around him, ate a surprisingly good piece of meat that neither looked nor tasted anything like those big turkey legs at a Ren Faire, and tried not to stare at Marian.

It wasn't easy.

He caught her looking back a few times, once even smiling when their unwanted companions asked about her marital state. His father had always claimed that *to listen is the greatest skill a man, or woman, could possess.* He should try it more.

Uncle Ross was such a badass that, despite hurling several subtle and not-so-subtle insults at their new English friends, he had earned their respect and even reverence by the end of the meal. Greyson had learned something else too. He'd seen more of the other side of Marian—the woman who was sick of following her father's rules. The spunky woman who might just turn those rules on their head if given the chance.

Not for the first time, he found himself wondering how she would do in the future. He could imagine her flourishing there, just as his mother had. And not only because it would free her from her dipshit fiancé's thumb. He liked the thought of her sitting across from him at a wrought iron table tasting a beignet for the first time after a walk through City Park.

"You've a quiet one among you," the talkative Englishman said, looking straight at him.

Never, not once in all his life, had he been accused of being quiet. Forthright, at best. Under his father and brother's shadow, at worst. But quiet? He'd love for his brothers to get a load of that one.

He tried to emulate the speech of his clan. Or his mother's clan. Whatever. "You were speaking of the reivers earlier, aye?"

Greyson couldn't look at Marian's face. He could tell she was holding back laughter at his poor attempt to sound Scottish, and if he saw her smirk, it wouldn't help matters.

"We were."

"And your disbelief the men were, indeed, English?"

Ross gave him a look of warning. They'd made nice, but he could ruin that with a few ill-placed comments.

Before the man could answer, Greyson continued. "I find disbelief of the horrors committed by our fellow humans a fairly ignorant stance." And that was the kindest word Greyson could think of after the dandy had ogled Marian all night. "The mind of man is capable of anything."

He tried not to smile. This was sort of fun. Like cosplaying, only with infinitely higher stakes.

"The most any of us could hope for is some knowledge of ourselves and, since that usually comes too late, a crop of inextinguishable regrets."

Thankfully, Joseph Conrad wasn't born yet and couldn't

complain that Greyson may have butchered his quote a bit.

The Englishman wasn't the only one unsure of how to respond. Forcing himself not to smile at his private joke, Greyson took a chance at breaking protocol.

"It appears some guests are taking advantage of the fine music to dance. Shall we, my lady?"

When none seemed to flinch at his request, Greyson breathed a bit easier. He might not fully understand thirteenth-century protocol, but he did know how to *mind his manners*, as his mother would say. And those manners seemed to come in handy now. Marian stood as he made his way toward her.

Even better?

Medieval nobles weren't prudes, at least. The dancers held each other closer than he'd ever dared to hold a partner at a formal event. His hands itched to touch her, to pull her close, but there were more than a few reasons for him to calm the fuck down.

She was engaged.

They'd be dropping her off soon with her future husband.

No to mention, he was from the future. With any luck, Greyson would not be staying here for very long.

But none of those things seemed to matter, or at least they didn't change his reaction to her. As they joined the other dancers and he took Marian into his arms, his heart raced and his pants tightened. Seeing her like this, in her element . . .

"Greyson"—Marian lowered her voice as she whispered into his ear—"I have a confession to make."

That did nothing to calm his pulse. If her confession was that she wanted to return to her chamber and have wild, passionate sex with him, he was pretty sure all of the reasons he shouldn't would mean squat.

"What is it?" He pulled back enough to ask. And probably shouldn't have done it. Hell, he definitely shouldn't continue to look at her this way.

"I am enjoying . . ."

You. I'm enjoying being with you.

"The freedom of being without a guardian. Exploring this grand castle, speaking to whomever I choose. 'Tis wonderful, really."

Damn.

"As you should. Have you ever been without one before?"

He knew the answer before she gave it. Greyson couldn't imagine such a leash on his life. The board of directors, and the press, were bad enough. But to have someone literally following him everywhere he went? No, thank you.

"Nay. My father could be a difficult man at times."

"At times?" She was being generous.

Marian laughed. "Many times," she agreed.

Screw it.

He pulled her as close as some of the other dancers. And here Greyson thought he could dance.

"You do this well, for a woman so sheltered. And I mean no offense."

"I shall take none, as I was sheltered indeed. 'Twas one of my father's good qualities, his affinity for music and dance."

They slid around the dance floor, gaining what was probably too much attention. But he was feeling reckless. Too reckless. He saw it in her eyes when they caught his ever so briefly. She knew his thoughts but didn't seem to be as wary of them as she should.

Lord help him.

"I have a confession too."

"Oh?"

He spun her in a move that had no place here. It did, in fact, garner more looks than he should be comfortable with. But Marian's happiness encouraged him.

"I am enjoying this day too."

13

His hands boldly explored parts of her body that no man had ever touched. They moved from her waist up toward her breasts, his mouth finally lowering to hers, hard and yet soft. She'd been dreaming of this kiss, of how Greyson's lips would feel on hers.

A loud knocking at the door forced its way into her mind.

Marian's eyes fluttered opened. It had been a dream, which was the only place where such a kiss could ever happen.

Disappointment threatened to choke her. But it was tempered by memories of the previous evening, of dancing with Greyson. Marian had told him about her day of freedom, and how much she'd enjoyed it. Dancing with him had been like a sweetmeat to a wonderful meal. In truth, yesterday had been one of the best days of her life. Holding James's head in her arms, the life gone from his eyes. That had been the worst.

He hadn't laughed at her at all. But he had laughed after confessing to having quoted a famous author to that pompous fool they'd been forced to dine with last eve. She'd asked for him to offer more *quotations*, as he called them, and he'd rattled off one after another, all attributed to famous people she'd never heard of. Because, he said, they did not yet exist. She remembered, particularly, a man named Shakespeare and a woman named Toni something that his mother liked. He'd seemed so certain, and the writings he'd spoken of were so wildly different . . .

Could it be possible? Could he really have traveled through time?

"My lady?"

The maid from last eve peered her head inside the door.

"Apologies for waking you, my lady. But your companions asked me to help ready you."

Reacting to her panicked tone, Marian jumped out of bed.

"They are leaving—"

"Immediately, my lady. Master Ross advised me to tell you they are already gathered in the courtyard."

Allowing the maid to assist her, Marian quickly dressed, wondering what had happened. After Greyson had told her of Yearger Irvine, she'd assumed they would stay at least long enough to await his return. She assumed Greyson's uncle had already done his duty as envoy for the Guardians of Scotland. As for Clan MacKinnish's real reason for visiting the castle?

She doubted it would be resolved so easily.

"Come, my lady," the maid said, rushing to the door. "They advised me to make haste." Four servants waited outside the chamber, apparently there to gather her trunks. "Master Greyson asked that I remind you to stay with your belongings until he can secure them," she said.

Marian watched as both trunks were lifted and carried from the chamber. As she followed them through the dimly-lit corridors, she tried to imagine what could possibly have happened this morn. No answer came to her. By the time they made their way out into the courtyard, Marian unable to even thank their host, the others were all mounted, ready to leave. All except her.

Two of Ross's men rushed forward to secure her trunks on a cart as Greyson rode up beside her with a horse.

"I'll explain on the road," he said. "Can you ride quickly?"

"Aye."

They hardly waited for her to mount before they started to move out. The sun was just beginning to rise as they made their way across Quinting Castle's courtyard. Wide open meadows and grass glistening with morning dew greeted them. She'd hoped to get Greyson's explanation sooner rather than later, but their speed prevented it. Finally, as they slowed to climb a ridge, Greyson fell in beside her.

"Irvine has allies in the castle. He must have gotten word we were here, according to one of Bruce's allies here at court. Ross didn't want to raise their suspicions by riding ahead, but now that we're out of sight . . ." He spoke quickly, darting glances at Ross and another of his men at the head of their small party. The two looked impatient. ". . . a few of us are going to ride ahead."

She must have looked worried because Greyson rushed to explain, "Ross assures me you will be safe on Quinting property. We'll join you as soon as possible."

"Greyson!" Ross yelled.

"I have to go." He pointed ahead at the next ridge as he rode away. "We'll find him and meet you soon. Don't worry, I promise you're safe."

And he was gone.

For the first time since the attack, Marian thought of her men lying in the road. Of the blood that had covered every one of them, the dead and their killers. Their avengers too. She thought of hiding in the bushes along the lake, certain she would not live out the day.

"My lady, ride with us. You have my word, you are safe here."

Alban, bless him.

She nodded and, with nothing else to do, followed.

They might be safe, but what about the others? If Greyson was truly from the future, did he know how to defend himself? Skill with the crossbow would not help in hand-to-hand combat.

From the future. Was she truly entertaining such a thought? Did it matter? She did not wish for Greyson to meet the same fate as poor Sir James. And if they did find this Yearger Irvine, he would not be alone.

And from what she understood, the man was not a man at all but a monster.

Marian shuddered.

IF HE'D THOUGHT BEING NAMED president of McCaim Shipping was playing in the big leagues, it paled in comparison to this. Chasing after a man on uneven and unfamiliar terrain was a bit different than riding for pleasure. And he hadn't ridden much in years, not since Mom's disappearance. It was more her passion than any of theirs, except Ian.

This entire morning had been a complete shitshow.

He'd thought a 5:00 a.m. wake-up to hit the gym before work was early, but Greyson had nothing on his uncle. Ross had apparently risen before sunrise, only to learn Yearger had returned late the night before, learned of their presence, and taken off again.

Guilty as hell.

At least, that's how they'd both taken it. They hadn't wasted any time getting out of Dodge. Seeing Marian after last night, after their dance . . . it had been hard to leave her, but Ross assured him she was safe on Quinting land, especially with the regent in attendance. Still, he'd almost stayed behind—hell, Ross had encouraged him to, worried he'd slow them down—but Yearger Irvine had tried to kill his mother.

Not a chance in hell was he standing down.

He may take his father and brother's lead more often than he wanted, but Greyson was a competitive bastard, as Reikart liked to say. He'd find a way to keep up with his uncle. Or at least he'd assumed so before the actual chase. Given the way they were careening across the road, the man might actually get them killed.

And then he saw them.

Three men riding ahead of them, riding fast but not at the breakneck speed Ross had insisted on the entire morning. But it seemed to have paid off. The men looked back over their shoulders.

"They've spotted us," Ross yelled back.

And they had.

Greyson had no business riding this fast so out of practice. He certainly shouldn't be charging toward medieval warriors. But the pain his family had been through drove him forward—straight past his uncle. He ignored Ross's calls from behind him, charging forward until he was close enough to hear the pounding of the enemies' hoofbeats. From nowhere, his uncle thundered past him, rode up to the closest of the three and, before Greyson could register what he was doing, slashed at him while full-on galloping. But his opponent had been prepared. The sound of clanging metal rang out as the man blocked the blow. Irvine's party slowed and then stopped, finally turning to face them.

So much for innocent until proven guilty.

His crazy uncle was already off his horse. Did he plan to take on all three of them alone?

Apparently.

Greyson had strung the bow this morning in preparation and didn't waste any time dismounting. Thankfully, the men weren't wearing any armor. Assuming shooting position, he nocked the arrow, drew, and anchored the bow. He aimed at the man farthest away from his uncle—he was a good shot but wasn't taking any chances under these circumstances, and with this bow—and released.

The fucker went down with a howl.

But Greyson didn't even pause. By the time he was ready to take a second shot, the two remaining men dropped their swords.

Running toward them for truer aim, Greyson stopped and prepared a second arrow, stopping short of drawing. In the movies, archers stood aimed and ready, but in reality, his arm would be shaking in no time with the effort. But he'd hold strong, whatever it took. They would have their answers.

"Which of you is Yearger?" his uncle yelled.

The coward on the ground, holding his stomach, looked right at their mark. Greyson could tell the man was tall and heavily muscled despite the fact that he lay on the ground. Just as he had the thought, the man began to rise.

"Shona MacKinnish."

It was all Ross said to him, and it didn't take long for his reaction. Or the reaction of his companion. The one with an arrow sticking out of his stomach was too busy bleeding to bother with his friends. Both jerked their heads toward his uncle, the name clearly familiar to them.

"Your friend will die without assistance," Greyson added. He had no idea if it were true. But just last week, he'd negotiated a contract making McCaim Shipping the owners of the only LNG-powered container ship in the world. He'd succeeded in part because he'd bluffed his way through the answers he didn't know. Confidence moved mountains.

Another lesson from his father. One he'd never imagined using under these precise circumstances.

"Shona MacKinnish is missing," Yearger said boldly.

"No shit." He couldn't help it. But apparently that wasn't a curse these guys knew yet, because every one of them looked at Greyson.

Radiating impatience, Ross stalked over to Yearger and raised his sword to the man's throat.

"Talk, or die. I've no preference."

To his credit, Yearger didn't flinch. But his companion did.

"Don't even think about it," Greyson warned.

If he tried to flee, Greyson would be forced to let loose. And the guy was clearly considering it.

"What happened the night the king died?" Ross asked.

Yearger looked from him to Ross and back. He obviously knew who they were, otherwise he wouldn't have slunk off after just returning to Quinting. He had to know Ross wouldn't hesitate to kill him. A fact his uncle seemed inclined to remind him of.

Greyson imagined himself raising his arm and aiming straight for the man's heart. If he truly had tried to kill his mother . . .

"The tale I heard is a short one, if you care to hear it," Ross said on a growl.

Yearger said nothing.

"Yer sister forced Shona to send a message to King Alexander. On the way back to Kinghorn, you tried to stab her. Then one of your men spooked the king's horse, and he met his death off the side of the cliff. Two dead bodies you'd have claimed if Shona had not escaped."

Still, Yearger said nothing. Greyson had negotiated with the best of them, and this guy was good. His body language didn't betray him.

"Tell me another tale," Ross finished, "or you meet the same fate as the king you were sworn to protect."

The smug little shit actually smiled. "How about a tale of your other sister, Grace? The one who worked her black magic to help Shona disappear. Have you spoken to her? Your other sister?"

Ross's hands shook, ever so slightly. But Greyson could see it from where he stood. He looked to the companion, who remained silent. But unlike Yearger, he didn't hide his nervousness.

"On whose orders did you implicate my sister in the king's death?" Ross asked.

"Do the Guardians know?" Yearger shot back. "They sent you as envoy to England, so surely not. But if they learned of your sister's involvement in the king's death . . ."

Greyson concentrated on the companion, the biggest threat to his uncle at the moment. He couldn't take his eyes from him. Just like in an archery match, everything blacked out in the background. The man bleeding on the dirt road. The carefree call of the birds above them. All his attention was fixed on the two men who stood much too close to Ross. Even though they'd shed their swords, Greyson had no doubt they had other weapons at their disposal. All of these guys carried daggers with them, and usually more than just one.

"Maybe you should tell them," Yearger said. "The Guardians and the Bruce. Shall we pay a visit to Scone together?"

Greyson could hear his heart beating. The fucker was threatening his aunt in an attempt to blackmail his uncle.

Yearger crossed his arms in defiance. And that's when Greyson realized this man would give them nothing. Apparently a few hundred years didn't matter much when dealing with the nature of man. Arrogant and overconfident, this guy thought he was Ross's superior. He had a pair, for sure, and he wasn't going to budge.

Unless they made him.

Carefully preparing the bow without drawing attention to himself, Greyson did take aim then—at Yearger's friend, the only one who might actually give them some information today. The man had been twitching since he'd dropped his weapon.

"You have five seconds to start talking," he said. "And I don't miss."

As evidenced by the third guy, who'd stopped screaming. Not a good sign.

"Five . . . four . . . three . . ."

The guy moved away from Yearger, and Greyson followed him with the bow. Encouraging.

"Two . . ."

"He tried to kill her," the man blurted out. "And took Lady Grace too. Kidnapped her at Kinghorn when she returned looking for Shona."

Greyson had no idea what he was talking about, but he wasn't surprised the man was talking. Fear could be a powerful motivator.

"Where is Grace?" Ross roared.

"It was the baron. The king. They made us do it."

"Nigel!" Yearger yelled.

The king? What in the ever-loving . . .

"Edward recruited you to kill King Alexander?" Ross asked incredulously. "And where are my sisters?"

In his entire life, Greyson had never witnessed such a display of anger. Ross's voice was like acid, his face bright red with veins popping out every which way, but his arm held steady . . . He was going to kill Yearger.

Greyson's mark moved quickly, backing away from Ross and Yearger and reaching for his sword. But just as Greyson prepared to make good on his threat, he realized his mark wasn't moving in for an attack on Ross. He was running away. Yearger, on the other hand, was grasping his lower thigh.

Greyson didn't hesitate.

He shot and Yearger fell.

As Greyson ran forward, Ross finished what he'd started.

His sword sliced through Yearger as easily as Greyson's arrow had done, and the dagger in Yearger's hand fell to the ground.

By the time he'd shifted his aim and was prepared to shoot again, the man named Nigel was already riding away. Ross didn't hesitate, and as they scrambled back to their horses, Greyson securing his bow behind him, he took one last look at the bodies.

Bodies of the men he'd killed. Well, he'd had help with one of them.

His stomach roiled. But he held off emptying the contents of his stomach, reminding himself that he'd avenged his mother. By the time the nausea passed, he didn't need Ross to tell him the companion had already gotten away.

This is turning out to be a particularly shitty day.

14

THEY'D BEEN RIDING all day. Ross and Greyson had not yet returned, but thankfully they hadn't met anyone else on the road. Though Alban spoke to Marian periodically, most often when they stopped to rest the horses, the rest of the men had remained mostly silent. There was a sense of nervous anticipation in the group.

They slowed as they came to a bridge with two guards, alongside a small pele tower. Marian realized the significance. After paying a toll to cross, they would no longer be under the protection of the king's regent. Fenwall would be to their southeast, the location of their attack directly to the north. But Marian was tossed around now and knew not what lay ahead, aside from danger.

"We stop here," Alban said just before the bridge.

Marian assumed they'd only halted to pay the toll, but the others dismounted too, one of them asking for her hand. After a brief discussion with the two guards, and an exchange of coin—or so she assumed—Alban rejoined their group.

"We wait for Ross and Greyson here."

At Marian's questioning look, he explained, "Ross said to wait for them at the edge of the regent's property."

He looked distinctly aggrieved at the suggestion. Marian puzzled over it for a moment until the answer dawned on her. Ross, or Greyson, or maybe both, did not want her to be without them outside of the regent's land. Which implied they did not trust the others to keep her safe.

She couldn't help but be secretly pleased. Of course she trusted Alban and the rest—they seemed quite capable—but no one made her feel safer than Greyson. And if this journey had taught her anything, it was that she needed protection more than she cared to admit.

If only it did not have to be that way.

Many times she'd asked her father to train her as he would have if she'd been a boy. He scoffed at her, of course. But that had not stopped her from asking.

"You can make use of the tower for your needs," Alban said, cutting into her thoughts.

She thanked him and then the guards, who'd likely first given the offer. It was like the others she'd seen along the border. Tall and compact, the hall akin to a large room with one single spiral staircase leading to the upper chambers.

With a bit of exploring, she found the garderobe quite easily, but after seeing to her needs, she found herself wishing to sit on something other than her horse. So she made use of a wooden chair, its seat made of leather, in the great room.

Marian's mind dipped back to the horror of losing James and the others, but she forced it away again, trying to muse about the future. About life as Duncan's wife. Her mind would not accommodate her though. It kept returning to him.

How easily his smile had come during their dance. The thrill of his hand on hers, his fingers warm and strong. And his claim. That black box that had reflected Marian's own image back to her.

He claimed to know things that had not yet happened, and when he spoke, the ideas made sense. But could he really be from the future? She struggled to believe it . . . and not to believe it. All she knew was that he was in danger, and she feared for him, feared she would never see him again, or that she would only see him as she had last seen James.

"Marian?"

So strong was her relief that Marian actually envisioned herself running up to Greyson and embracing him. Instead, she stood and walked toward him as she'd been trained to do. Slow, back straight, a proper lady.

"I worried for you and your uncle," she admitted.

I was terrified you wouldn't return. The thought made me sadder than it should have given we hardly know each other.

It took her a moment to realize he'd worried for her too. She hadn't noticed his tone when he'd called her name, too relieved to think of anything else, but the way he looked at her now . . . there was no doubt as to what he had been thinking.

"I didn't like leaving you. I worried for you," he replied, the simple words holding more meaning than he'd probably intended.

"Did you find him?"

"We did."

When he didn't elaborate, Marian grasped her hands together and squeezed. She shouldn't be thinking of their dance, but she couldn't seem to stop herself. She wanted him to touch her, to pull her into his arms.

"Is he still alive?"

At first, she didn't see Greyson shaking his head. When she did, the insides of Marian's cheeks stung. It was in that moment, as she watched the confusion and pain that he did not even attempt to hide, that Marian knew the truth.

He was a big, strong man unaccustomed to the violence and death around him. Much like he'd seemed out of sorts at last night's dinner. Add in his strange speech, his claims, that image of her, the blank look he gave her now . . .

"You are not from this time?"

It should have been impossible. And yet . . .

"No, I am not."

Marian reeled at the thought, even though she'd been considering it for days now. This man had been so intent on finding and protecting his family, he'd traveled not just to a foreign place but to a different time. And now he was out of place. Lost.

She didn't think.

Because if she'd put any thought into throwing herself into a man's arms, one who was neither a relative nor her betrothed, she would not have done it. But it felt more right than anything ever had. When he wrapped his own arms around her, Marian tightened her grip on him, holding him even more tightly than she had that first time.

She'd been in danger then.

Now it was his turn.

Greyson was in danger of coming undone. But she would not let him.

"Tell me," she said, resting her face sideways on the very top of his chest. Though she could feel only the soft fabric of his linen shirt and tunic, Marian breathed in deeply, unused to such a clean scent. He bathed nearly every day, sought out water as if the other place he'd hailed from was a great ocean.

But this was no fish she held. He was pure man.

"I killed his companion," Greyson said, his tone flat. "We caught up with them on the road, and Ross charged ahead. My mother was so happy when I learned archery. She was the one who gave me the idea. But I never"—his voice caught—"I never intended . . ."

Her arms tightened around him.

"I shot Yearger too. But his friend admitted he was guilty.

That Yearger helped kill the king and tried to stab my mother. I don't know if I killed him."

Greyson was not making sense.

"What did his friend do?"

He was quiet for a moment. "The companion's name was Nigel. He played his own role. When Grace returned to Hightower, she said Shona had inadvertently played a part in the king's death, but Nigel and another guard named Loxton were the ones who did the deed. Then Yearger followed her back to the castle, trying to kill her."

Marian pulled back enough to see his face.

"And Nigel confirmed all of this?" she asked in wonder. "Why?"

Greyson took a deep breath, so deep she could feel his chest rise and fall under her own.

"I had an arrow pointed at his heart. The tip of Ross's sword sat at Yearger's throat. Nigel said they'd been recruited by some baron, by the king."

Her eyes widened.

"*Your* king," he specified unnecessarily.

Their faces were just inches apart.

"King Edward recruited some baron, who in turn recruited the Irvine family to"—she could hardly believe it—"kill King Alexander? Why did they involve your mother?"

But Marian didn't need him to answer. The truth suddenly seemed obvious. "As a scapegoat. Which makes sense. Clan MacKinnish is known to support the Bruce. To implicate him in King Alexander's death would effectively eliminate him as a successor to the Crown."

Greyson nodded. "Edward wants the Scottish crown?" he asked.

She thought about it for a moment. "But 'tis impossible. He has recognized Scotland's independence. His regent just accepted the Guardians of Scotland's decree proclaiming the Maid of Norway as the successor."

And yet it made sense. She believed it was true, all of it.

"Did any of them live?" she asked.

"Nigel got away. The other two are dead." From the way he said it, she knew he felt it keenly, in a way few warriors would.

There were still so many questions. But none of them seemed as important at the moment as the fact that she was standing in a guardhouse in the arms of a man who was, quite literally, from the future. A man who'd made her feel things no other man ever had.

"I am with you."

She meant it in the same way as the sentiment he'd offered her in the woods that first night. It was a message that she understood, if only a little, how he felt. She knew what it was to be in a place you did not belong.

But when she said it, the thickness of her voice betrayed her. His expression told her he knew what she meant. He knew what was actually in her heart.

Greyson's cheeks moved as his jaw tightened, indecision gripping him as surely as it did her.

"I have no right to do this."

His head lowered toward hers. As it did, Marian's dream floated through her mind. But this was no dream. Greyson was about to kiss her.

She wanted him to as surely as she wanted this journey to last forever.

His lips, so soft and warm, touched hers.

Marian pressed back, the moment made so much sweeter for the vulnerability he allowed her to witness. But this was not a kiss for him. Or for her.

It was one for them both.

And over much too soon.

Greyson pulled back and opened his mouth to speak, but she'd never know what he had been prepared to say.

His uncle, on the other hand, did not hold back his displeasure.

"Greyson!"

She jumped away immediately. What must he think of her?

It was just a small portion of what she thought of herself. Marian raced past Ross and right out of the hall. Pressing her back against the stone wall, she lifted a hand to her chest. Her heart pounded underneath, as evident as if her hand touched bare skin.

She knew in that moment that she could never go back to the way things were before. This moment had forever changed her.

15

"Riders."

There were only three of them, but as soon as she saw them, Marian thought of her men. Just like that day, she suddenly found herself surrounded, Greyson among those who protected her.

They had hardly spoken since the day before, Ross no doubt being the cause, but he'd never been far from her thoughts. Although she kept reminding herself of her duty to her father, her heart longed for the feeling of freedom she'd experienced at Quinting Castle. For the way she'd felt in Greyson's arms.

"Stay close," Greyson said, reaching for his bow.

As their party stopped to greet the newcomers, he also reached inside the quiver at his side. Shedding blood was difficult for him, but she did not doubt he would do it to protect her. She only prayed it wasn't necessary. They'd passed the border earlier in the day. It mattered not these men were Scottish. The only alliance in the Marches was to yourself and your clan, Ross had reminded all of them. *Be leery*, he'd said.

Ross moved forward to speak with the leader.

Marian could not hear what was being said, but the other

men seemed to relax a bit as they spoke. Except for Greyson. He never let go of either bow or arrow. If he truly had traveled back to the past, he'd adapted to their ways quickly.

Then, nearly as quickly as they'd come upon them, the riders passed them. Marian watched as the three men, one with a cart trailing behind his horse, continued on their way.

Ross stopped just next to Greyson.

"We've a problem."

As stone-faced as the others, Greyson did not react. Was it her imagination, or did he look more and more like them each day? He had a bit of scruff on his face now, and the hardened look of a man prepared to defend himself and his people, whatever it took. She doubted anyone would look at the group of men and single him out.

Until he spoke, of course.

"Bruce, the damned fool, has come out in open revolt against Balliol," Ross blustered. "He's taken his castle at Dumfries and sits now at Buittle Castle in Galloway."

"Took Balliol's lordship? Is he mad?" a man named Brodie asked. The largest of them all, Brodie had a full beard and bushy eyebrows.

Greyson didn't ask any questions, but Marian could see the confusion on his face. She took it as further proof that his story was true. It was simply not possible for a relative of MacKinnish not to understand the implications of Bruce's actions. Even she, kept out of discussions on politics due to her very delicate nature, or so her father claimed . . . even *she* understood.

"Worse, James the Steward is with him."

Brodie cursed, and Greyson looked even more confused than before.

"They had the support of the Earl of Menteith."

Alban shook his head. "Fools. They do it for Edward's benefit."

Marian paused at that. Edward's benefit? Why would the

King of England . . . ahh, she understood now. They hoped to show the King of England they were willing to fight for their country, if needed. They postured for future support. She gave Greyson a look that said she would explain later.

"They must be stopped. I must tell the Bruce our message has been accepted by the English regent."

A mumble of "ayes" followed.

Ross looked at Greyson. "You will take Lady Marian to Duncan and speak with his father. Tell him we've gone to Galloway to stop the Bruce. I will take two men with me. The others remain to guard our lady."

And my coin.

He didn't say it, but Marian knew the trunk needed guarding even more than her person.

"We meet at Hallstead Manor in Cumbernauld. 'Tis as good a place as any to meet before traveling north to Hightower."

Marian didn't understand the look that passed between Greyson and his uncle, but it had something to do with her. She was sure of it.

"My men will show you the way," Ross said to Greyson. "Stay close to them."

With that, he and his chosen companions departed. Those remaining looked at each other as if wondering who would take charge.

Greyson was the first to speak.

"I don't know the area, but I do know we're in more danger every passing minute. Show me the way."

The men nodded, not questioning him.

Greyson and Marian fell behind the others, riding side by side. Every so often, she caught a glimpse of Ross much further ahead of them. Unencumbered, he traveled more quickly. Confident the others could not hear her, she allowed herself to speak frankly with Greyson.

"Who are you, in your life, to command the others so naturally?"

"My title would be unfamiliar to you, but my family runs a business, a shipping company. My father started it from nothing and now it's one of the largest in the world."

Marian shifted in her saddle. "You have great admiration for him."

Greyson's smile faltered. She waited for a response, but he didn't give her one. She should let it go . . .

"You said he was in a coma, but the word is unfamiliar to me. Something about sleep?"

Greyson's shoulders rose and fell, as if from a swell of emotion, but he did respond this time.

"An infection"—he frowned—"it's like he's sleeping but may never wake again. He's being kept alive by machines."

Anyone would be troubled to see a loved one in such distress, and yet, she sensed there was more to it. Something else was troubling Greyson. "You miss him?"

Finally, he looked at her, his gaze stormy. "We treated him poorly."

Marian didn't understand.

"When he told us his theory about Mom being pulled back in time . . . we thought he'd made the whole thing up, even the story Mom had told him. But with each passing year, he became more and more obsessed. He stopped letting us go into his study, and we let him." His jaw flexed. "Rhys and I all but forced him to step down from the company after the board demanded it. He'd always planned to make my brother the CEO, and I'd already been named COO the previous year. But it shouldn't have happened that way."

Marian didn't have much experience with a loving father, but she knew what Gilda would say.

"We sometimes hurt the people we love, but it is precisely because they love us that allows us to make amends."

Greyson shook his head. "I wouldn't blame him if he woke up and kicked all four of us from his hospital room." He finally smiled at her, a slight quirk of his lips. "And we'd all leave, except for Ian. That boy has no idea how to take directions."

"Boy? How old is he?"

"Twenty-seven."

She worked out the strange way he told his brother's age.

"Rhys is the oldest, then Reikart and I are Irish twins."

"I thought you were Scottish?"

Greyson laughed. "It's an expression. We're close in age, born within a year of each other. I'm thirty; he's twenty-nine."

"How wonderful to have so many siblings."

"Pfft. Not always. They're a pain in my ass most of the time."

His expression didn't match his words. He obviously loved them very much. What Marian wouldn't give to be a part of such a family. To be loved that way.

The beginning of an idea formed.

Nay. It was not possible.

"Do you think you'll be able to get back to them? Provided they do not all come here?"

The others slowed in front of them, preventing Greyson from answering.

"'Tis a good place to feed and rest the horses," one of the men said.

Marian could hear the water to their right, but she couldn't see it. She assumed they had followed a river north. Marian supposed it made sense.

Their small party dispersed, two men taking the horses through the thicket toward the water. Two others rummaged through the bags on the cart, presumably for some scraps of food.

"Shall we take ours to the water as well?" Marian asked, dismounting.

"Let's do it."

She wasn't sure exactly when it had happened, but any final doubts Marian had felt about Greyson had been laid to rest. Every time he spoke now, she heard something that gave him away. The words he chose sometimes, or the way he pronounced things.

Greyson was from the future.

"You're looking at me weird."

Precisely. Like that.

"Am I?"

There was no sign of the other men, but as they approached the river bank, her horse balked. She stopped, walked him in a circle, and approached again. By the time she got him to the river bank, Greyson's mount had already drunk his fill.

The sun peeked out then, as if rewarding her efforts. Marian lifted her face toward it and closed her eyes. When she felt the brush of Greyson's fingers against her hand, she let him take her horse's lead. Keeping her eyes closed, savoring the stillness of the moment, she took a deep breath and felt a rush of simple contentment.

When she looked again, he was standing just next to her, the horses tied behind them to a tree. Standing this close, she was reminded of how large he was—but instead of intimidating her, it made her feel protected.

"I never knew my mother," she said, looking into a pair of contemplative blue eyes. "I wonder what she would have said of the thoughts that ran through my head now?"

"Tell me your thoughts."

Could she really verbalize them?

Aye, to him she could.

"I don't want to become Duncan's wife."

He didn't hesitate. "Then don't."

Even if a small part of her had expected his answer, it still startled her.

"I have no choice. But at Quinting, I felt so free. No one to watch my every move. As if"—she felt silly now—"as if anything were possible."

He continued to watch her, and Marian realized she spoke nonsense. Shaking her head, she attempted to walk away.

But a hand stopped her.

Not just any hand. His hand.

And this was no innocent touch.

16

He was a fucking idiot.

His life was a cluster at the moment. Somehow he'd managed to embroil himself in the assassination of a king while every single member of his family was in danger. But here he was, about to make yet another monumental mistake.

Didn't matter. He couldn't stay away from her anymore. Every time they touched, Greyson felt it.

A connection unlike anything he'd ever experienced. But until now, their connection had been innocent. A comforting touch.

Yeah right.

He had no right to entwine his fingers with hers. No right to grasp her hand as if he'd never let go. And he definitely had no right to be thinking the kind of thoughts that were running through his head at this very moment.

"Anything is possible," he said softly, "in my time."

Something had cracked between them, some wall. The teasing tone had left Marian's voice when she asked him about the future. She believed him now. And the way she was looking at him . . .

She'd gone from skeptic, rightly so, to believer a hell of a lot faster than he and his brothers had made the leap.

"In my time, women choose their own husbands. They have the same rights as men, although there's still some work to do, admittedly. But you'll be pleasantly surprised by the differences, I think."

"I cannot . . . are you proposing . . . ?"

"I'll take you back. After we find my mother and brother, or brothers, if I can go back—"

"*If* you can go back. And if you can't?"

All hell would break loose? Greyson didn't know, exactly, but he did know one thing: Marian deserved more than what she was getting. And if he had his way, he'd give it to her.

"We'll figure it out. Sometimes you just have to take the leap and let it work itself out."

"I am not your burden to bear," she said softly.

In response, Greyson took her other hand, threading his fingers through hers. Holding both of her hands, he sought her gaze. When he found it, he said, "You're far from a burden, Marian. You are strong and capable. You don't need anyone, including me, to make it in the future. I'm not trying to tie you down. If we can get back, I'll be anything you want me to be. Your friend. Someone to help you find your way."

Shit. That wasn't exactly what he wanted. But he didn't want to make his offer sound conditional either. If she wanted him to stand back, he would. Because . . .

"You deserve a bit of freedom," he added.

That did it. He could see it in her eyes.

"Say the words. Say you'll come with me."

Because if she did, if Marian agreed, she'd no longer be an engaged woman. Which meant he would be free to kiss those lips he'd been staring at nonstop. Jesus, he wanted to kiss her so much. He'd been desperate to kiss her ever since that first day. But he couldn't. Not unless she said the words.

"My father's alliance . . ."

"Fuck your father's alliance." He squeezed her hand. "And I won't apologize for saying it. Neither should you. Say what you're feeling, Marian, and make no apologies. Say it."

"I . . . I don't want to marry Duncan."

"And?"

"I want to be free."

He could hear his heartbeat in his ears. "Say it."

She looked into his eyes as she answered his call. "I'll come with you."

Greyson brought his head down, thankfully remembering at the very last moment she probably hadn't made out with many men. He wanted to ravage her mouth, but instead he moved slowly.

Pressing his lips to hers, he waited for her permission to continue. When she let go of his hands, only to wrap them around his waist, he grasped both sides of her face. Sliding his tongue along the crease of her lips, he willed them open.

Ignoring the state of his extremely hard cock, or at least trying to, Greyson showed her what to do next. He coaxed her mouth wider, willing her to touch her tongue to his.

When she finally did, he was lost.

He drank from her sweetness, her strength. He willed his hands to stay where they were, not wanting to scare her by allowing them to wander. But with every movement of her mouth, with every press of their tongues, he wanted more.

So much more, it terrified the hell out of him. He'd never felt this out of control with a woman before.

What a stupid, idiotic promise he'd made. To take her back and set her free? As if he wouldn't slam his fist in the face of the first man she kissed, other than him.

I want to be free.

He'd do well to remember it. Still, Greyson couldn't stop. At least not until the neighing of her skittish horse interrupted them. Reminding him of where they were, and what they had to do next.

Shit.

Pulling away, he let his hands linger on her face, cupping it as he looked into her eyes, waiting for her to change her mind.

But she wouldn't. He understood the resolve there. It was a feeling he knew well.

"That was enjoyable."

He ruined the moment by letting go of her face, by laughing at the beautiful simplicity of her words.

"I should hope so."

Thankfully, she smiled too.

"Can we do it again?"

He took her hand, leading them to the horses.

"That's what freedom means, Marian. You can do whatever the hell you want. If you want to kiss me, go for it. If you want to tell me to fuck off, you can do that too."

Reluctantly letting her go once again, Greyson started untying their horses from the tree.

"Your uncle won't be pleased. I'm not sure you understand the implications."

With both horses untied, they faced each other.

"Which is probably a good thing."

Marian rolled her eyes. "Duncan's father is one of your Guardians. He's a powerful man, more powerful than my father even."

Yeah, he didn't really want to know all of that. Not because he wanted to be ignorant of the potential fallout, but because it didn't matter. She had made her decision, and Greyson would do whatever was necessary to support that. Period. End of story. She'd been treated like a pawn for her entire life, and it was time for that shit to stop.

He smiled. "Apparently my family is pretty powerful too. What kind of woman survives an attack by the same man complicit in the murder of a king? Or consorts with fae to devise a way to send her sister through time? We'll worry about Ross's reaction, and your father's and your fiancé's, when we need to. For now, let's concentrate on getting to Hallstead Manor in one piece."

"I think we have a more immediate concern." Marian nodded her head, indicating he should turn around.

So he did.

And cursed under his breath.

17

ALBAN HAD SEEN THEM.

And was walking toward them with a grimace that would have made Ross proud. Marian stepped forward, prepared to apologize and beg forgiveness for such untoward behavior.

"Before you say anything, she's no longer betrothed. We head straight for Hallstead Manor." Greyson's words did not invite a response.

"If we do not take her to the Earl of Fife . . ." Alban's words trailed off as he looked from her to Greyson.

That's what freedom means. You can do whatever the hell you want.

It sounded so sweet, but at what cost? For she had no doubt both her father and the Scottish earl would look for her. If either found her, Marian might wish for death instead of the punishment she would find for abandoning her duty.

A duty she'd never wanted.

Or asked for.

But one that had hung over her for as many years as she'd been alive.

"My lady?"

Alban could likely sense her hesitation. But he mistook the reason for it. Despite the danger, Marian would risk everything for the chance to feel as she had at Quinting Castle. As she did with Greyson's lips pressed to hers.

She hesitated because of something else Greyson had said.

Say what you're feeling, Marian, and make no apologies.

Marian had been about to do just that. Sharing a kiss with a man not her husband, or even her betrothed, was that not wrong? Marian was unsure what to say even if she owed no explanation.

"I wish to accompany you to Hallstead Manor," she said finally.

With a shake of his head, Alban walked away, leaving them alone again. Silently, they led their horses away from the river bank and toward the road.

"We'll figure this out together," Greyson said. And she'd never liked a word better than she liked that one. *Together.*

Marian could feel her cheeks warming as she looked at him.

In response, he winked at her just before they emerged from the thicket. For the remainder of the day, Marian alternated from panicked moments imagining her father's reaction when he learned she had not made it to Duncan to elation at the thought of not having to marry a man with such a horrible reputation.

And then there was Greyson.

By the time they reached the outskirts of the village of Kenfern, Marian knew more about this man from another time. Riding well behind the others across mostly flat marshland, they'd spoken easily well into the night.

He told her of his family, of the city where he was from. Of his father's business, which had been passed to the sons, and the toll his mother's disappearance had taken on all of them. But there were things Greyson did not say that Marian learned anyway.

He loved his family very much. Though he spoke of disagreements with each of them, Greyson obviously adored them all. Worry for them overshadowed even his fear at having been tossed into a time not his own. Finding his mother and brother, returning to his father—those were the only things that mattered to him.

How, precisely, did she fit into his plans?

"It looks like a movie set."

Marian was becoming accustomed to Greyson's strange words.

"Movie set?"

He glanced ahead, as if judging the distance to the others, and gave a small shake of his head. They were getting too close to speak freely anymore. "I'll tell you about that later."

"The owner of the Brable Inn is also Kenfern's alewife," Brodie said as they caught up to the rest of the group. "She'll be askin' questions."

He didn't have to explain. Even Greyson seemed to understand those questions would be about her.

"Seriously? She's been traveling with us for days with no problems."

"As the daughter of the Earl of Fenwall whose guards were killed, leaving her without escort."

Greyson shrugged. "And?"

Brodie and Alban exchanged a glance.

"'Tis an identity she can no longer take."

The men had obviously spoken amongst themselves about her situation. She'd thought about it too—of course she had—but her conversation with Greyson had been so thrilling, she'd been loath to cut it short to discuss the hard realities of their situation.

"Word will spread when I do not arrive to marry Duncan."

Greyson tipped his head. "Word of Lady Marian, or a

woman by another name. Does it matter when your companions are known?"

"I know only of the alewife by reputation," Brodie said. "We've not stayed here before."

She could see Greyson understood now.

"You'll all be taking on aliases to protect Marian?"

Marian raised her chin, addressing the men. Knowing it was time for her to do so.

"I lost those dear to me, and others loyal to my father. I've been bartered to secure an alliance between my father and his northern neighbors for reasons unbeknownst to me. You've done more to protect me than I can thank you for. But I cannot ask that you put yourselves in danger. Can we not avoid Kenfern Village?"

It was Brodie who answered. "We need supplies. And rest. None know us, or you, here. We vowed to keep you safe, and will do so, my lady."

It was more than she deserved.

"Call none by name," Alban said to the others. "And the lady is . . ." He looked to her for ideas, but Marian had no response.

"She is my wife." Greyson nodded toward the village. "I am Greyson McCaim and Marian is my wife."

Everyone looked at her.

Though she knew it was only a falsehood intended to pacify the innkeepers, Marian could not help the flutter inside her stomach.

"As he says."

Brodie repeated her words. "As he says."

With that, they rode on, moving past a waterwheel and a smithy and into the muddy roads between wooden buildings outlined in moonlight. Where before the smell was of woods and fresh air, here the scent was of roasting meat and wood fires.

As the two-story inn came into view, they slowed. Greyson

dismounted before she did, and Marian found herself reaching down to his outstretched hand.

"Mrs. McCaim," he said as she took his hand.

Though the term was unfamiliar to her, she understood what it signified.

And suddenly, the prospect of marriage she'd so long despised was no longer unwelcome. Pretending to be Greyson's wife would not be difficult. Indeed, she imagined it would prove to be just the opposite.

18

Being "married" to Marian was pure hell. More torturous than he could have possibly imagined.

The conversation at dinner, effortless, as it had been all day. But then they'd gone up to their room, which they'd have to share given their ruse, and it was smaller than his college dorm room.

He left her to change, finding the great room downstairs, though it wasn't so great, especially compared to their last lodgings at the castle, but the men had already gone off to their own sleeping area.

The men they traveled with were good men, he'd learned. Ones he could easily have been friends with back home. They joked around, just as his friends would have back home. Clansmen, according to Ross. And he was learning membership in a clan was nearly the same as being in a family. Sometimes they disagreed. Fought even. But these men would kill for Ross, for Marian, and even for him.

Literally kill. Not some metaphorical shit. Which was scary as hell, really.

Knowing the only bath that awaited him in the room was a

scented bowl of water with a cloth the size of a hand towel to dry, Greyson headed to the river as he'd done every time one was nearby. Thankfully, it was mostly quiet. Aside from a few squawking chickens and a woman tossing a bucket of water out of a back window of the inn, he didn't run into anyone.

When Ross had first caught him in the very illicit act of actually wanting to be clean, he'd warned him not to make it a habit. Apparently bathing wasn't always possible. Greyson couldn't wait to share that bit of irony with his mother.

He *would* see her again. He had to believe it.

As he stripped, preparing himself for the bitter cold, he allowed himself to imagine the reunion. With every day that passed, Greyson was more and more sure his mother was here. It made sense, his father's claim that she'd been pulled back. Aunt Grace must have found some way to summon her.

He still hadn't worked out the time travel rules exactly, but it seemed like travelers returning to their own time resurfaced close to the time of their disappearance. With luck, that meant when they returned not much time would have passed, just like when his mom had traveled back here.

Of course, his theory could be complete shit too.

If Mom had been pulled back, where was she? And where was Rhys? Would he find them at Perthshire, or had they already moved on?

And had Reikart and Ian found a way to follow them here?

The questions had been running through his mind over and over again, but he forced them out, knowing what he'd told Marian was true. They had to focus on staying alive, reaching Ross, and then finding his family.

But first things first. He needed to survive this night. Alone in a room with Marian.

Something told him that would be his biggest challenge yet.

The cold of the river hit him as it did every time. The coldest water that came through his faucet back home was like a sauna compared to the temperature of this water. Making quick work of a modified bath, Greyson dried and dressed again, then headed back to the inn as if it were the last few steps of a plank. No one prevented him from entering the hall, finding their room, and knocking on the door using the code word they'd set.

"Lagniappe."

He'd explained the concept of something "extra," a little bonus as it were, to Marian, one of many things he'd told her about his time. But there were so many things he still hadn't said. Most of it would just have to go without explanation until she could witness it for herself.

If they got back.

When she opened the door, Greyson swallowed. If he'd thought her fully clothed form a treat for his eyes, this was the whole damn bakery.

"Maid Marian."

From what he could tell, costume designers had gotten this one right. The nightgown-looking thing covered every inch of her, but somehow it was more erotic than any piece of lingerie he'd ever seen.

She typically wore her hair down, but tonight it was braided down her back.

More accessible in some ways, less in others. A woman whose life had been turned upside-down, but who was, for tonight, his wife.

In name only.

"You never did tell me that story," she said softly as she walked to the bed, the only bed, and sat. Clearly self-conscious, she tried to play off a calm he knew she didn't feel.

To be honest, neither did he. Greyson's heart was beating like a virgin's, the very thought of being alone, in a bedroom, with Marian heady enough that it was hard to walk. But walk he did, pulling out a simple wooden chair, careful not to knock over the two candles on the table beside it.

He was starting to become accustomed to the smell of smoke these candles gave off, although the ones in the castle had smoldered less. It couldn't be good for the lungs.

Straddling the chair to hide his obvious arousal, he leaned over the top of it, content just to watch her expression as it changed from apprehension to interest.

"It's a bit of English folklore. Robin Hood was an outlaw. A nobleman and an expert archer. He was known for stealing from the rich and giving to the poor." He smiled. "And for his beautiful lover, Maid Marian."

She cocked her head to the side, pretending to be thoughtful. "So she was beautiful, this Maid Marian?"

God, yes.

"The legends all say so. And confident. She apparently loved Robin Hood very much."

"Why do you suppose a woman like that should love a thief?"

"Ahh," he teased, "not just any thief. One who gave his earnings to those in need."

"'Tis still thievery."

"But for a purpose."

"Do you think he was in the right, then?"

He thought about it for a moment. "To love a beautiful, confident woman who returned his affections? Hell yes."

Marian rolled her eyes. "You know that's not what I meant."

The playfulness in her expression didn't do anything to dampen his amorous mood. This room was small and musty. But sitting at the bedside of this woman in candlelight, talking about Robin Hood . . . this was probably the most romantic thing he'd ever done.

Greyson wasn't Ian. He didn't wine and dine. When he made time for women, it was usually brief and never serious. Work consumed him. Proving himself to his father, to Rhys, had been his purpose for as long as he could remember.

But things were different here. Survival was the name of the game. Made one think a bit.

"I know what you meant. But I'd much prefer to talk about love than the merits of wealth redistribution."

"Have you been in love before?"

"No." He didn't even need to think about it. Lisa had been his longest relationship, and he'd never lost himself to her. Not even a little. The thought of comparing her even remotely to Marian was absurd.

He watched her carefully. "Have you?"

Marian shook her head. "I'm not allowed to fall in love."

He didn't mean to laugh, but it bubbled out of him. The hurt on her face drew Greyson up out of his chair. He sat next to her on the bed, his weight pulling them both down. With luck, the damn thing would hold. It didn't seem like the sturdiest thing ever.

"You are now."

He'd meant that she was free from Duncan. That she would be returning with him to a place where she could forge her own path. But he didn't correct himself. The idea of Marian being in love with him was undeniably pleasant.

"Where you're going, you can love anyone you'd like. You can be, or do, anything. No restrictions."

"Not even those of birth?"

His shoulders sank. Greyson's parents had worked damned hard to build McCaim Shipping, but the truth was he'd grown up privileged. His mother had insisted they work, always. They'd earned things like cars and cell phones from putting in time at the company. But he'd grown up in a mansion. Gone to Yale.

"The class system isn't gone," he admitted. "Some people are born into wealth, like me. Others, not so much. But there is opportunity too. And your heart—" He reached out without thinking, placing his hand over her chest. "Your heart is yours to give, or to keep."

Marian bit her lip, and he was lost.

"And if I choose to give it to you?"

His chest constricted.

"I would be honored," he said honestly.

Greyson waited, just a moment, to let his words sink in. And then he leaned forward, his hand still over her heart. When she closed her eyes in anticipation, Greyson had to will his body to stand down. Her lips, so soft and innocent. But this time she knew what to do. And when their kiss turned heated pretty damn quickly, she responded by opening for him.

Tongues tangling, Greyson tried to take it slow, reminding himself every sensation was new to her. But when Marian's hands moved to his head, pressing him closer to her, his tenuous grip on willpower gave way.

Their kiss quickly turned frantic, Greyson not even sure how she'd ended up lying under him. As he pressed against her, Marian did not hold back. Her moans encouraged him to trace his hand farther up her thigh.

"Can I lift your nightgown?" he asked, hating to pull away.

"Chemise."

He took that as a yes, and instead of resuming their kiss, he watched Marian's face as his hand moved higher and higher. Shifting his weight to the side to allow him room to maneuver her *chemise* up, he tried to figure out where to start.

What will give her the most pleasure?

An easy one, but Greyson wasn't sure she was ready for that. Instead, he trailed his hand up to one perfectly formed breast, covering it and squeezing gently. When his thumb rubbed over the nipple, Marian's mouth dropped just enough for him to be unable to resist.

Kissing her, hard, Greyson pinched and teased, unfortunately only able to reach one breast at the moment. Their kiss turned carnal and . . .

Fuck it.

Her lack of panties, another medieval boon, made it too damn easy. Repositioning them, he allowed his hand to wander, which was when Marian stopped him.

"Surely you will not touch me . . . there?"

"Not unless you want me to."

Her look of confusion reminded him of her lack of experience.

"It will feel good. I promise. But you're in charge here. Tell me to stop, I stop. Tell me you want more, and by God, Marian, I will give you everything. But it's up to you."

She still looked unsure. "We are unmarried."

"True. But it's not such a scandalous thing in my time, for two people to have sex outside of marriage."

His hand, splayed across her inner thigh, did not move an inch. But man, it wanted to.

"I think I'll like your time."

Greyson was deadly serious. "You will like this even more."

She nodded. He didn't hesitate.

The first touch of his fingers on her curls was as much of a shock to him as her. Why did everything feel better, more, with this woman?

"Part your legs for me, Marian," he said, trying to soften the edge of his tone. Greyson had always been accused of being assertive. Bedroom, boardroom, didn't matter.

She did. He pressed his finger inside.

But not like some clueless dipshit—his finger only a small part of the equation. Greyson used his thumb too, circling her nub as he moved in and out.

The expression on her face was everything.

"Like it?"

She opened her mouth, but when no sound escaped,

Greyson laughed. And kissed her then, relentless on every front. He would make her come so hard Marian would not only follow him to the twenty-first century, but she would choose him there too.

Her hips lifted to meet him, chemise bunched up around her chest, his impatience to see her pleasure evident. And when she cried out against his lips, it was like every deal he'd ever closed, every orgasm he'd ever experienced, all at once. He didn't let up until he could feel the clenching begin to subside.

What he wouldn't give to be inside her.

Unfortunately, he'd brought his cell phone, now dead, but no condoms.

Besides, this was all new to her. Making love to Marian and pulling out would be like if the Saints went to the Super Bowl and lost by one point.

After he adjusted her nightgown—chemise—he scooped her up beside him on the small bed, content to remain in his clothes if it meant lying just like this.

"You were right," she said, her head tucked into his chest.

"About?"

But he smiled, already knowing.

"I liked it. Very much."

Greyson groaned. "Just wait, Maid Marian, until the true lagniappe."

Except even as he said it, he knew the true unexpected gift wouldn't be them making love, but the fact that a woman like her had chosen to give herself to him.

And he was determined to earn it.

19

MARIAN'S EYES BLINKED OPEN, but she didn't dare move. She was tucked into Greyson's side, and he'd removed his tunic sometime in the night. Her hand lay on his bare chest, one she could see clearly in the bit of sunlight streaming through the mostly closed shutter. It was odd, and extremely pleasurable, to wake in such a position. Unable to resist, Marian ran her hand along the ridges of his stomach, across the markings there.

So many of them.

"Tattoos."

Her head snapped up. She hadn't realized he was awake.

"We call them tattoos."

"I've seen them before, though rarely, but I've never heard them called such a thing." She continued to trace the swirling images and words, grateful James had taught her to read. "Do you believe in Odin, then?"

The word *Valhalla* was splayed across the top of his chest.

"No. I got that on the one-year anniversary of my mother's disappearance." As he talked, one of Greyson's hands moved toward her back. "I was obsessed with Viking lore as a child. My mother would tease me, tell me perhaps I was Norse in another life." He must have pulled the string from the bottom of her braid as she could feel it being undone.

"None of us agreed on what had happened to Mom. But I was pretty sure she wasn't coming back. I knew I had to come to terms with that. I got that as a reminder we'd not meet again in my lifetime, that I would have to wait until another time and place to see her again."

He freed her braid completely.

"In Valhalla," she said.

"Or Heaven. Call it what you will. Seemed appropriate, like an inside joke. A twisted, sad inside joke between me and the mother I'd never see again."

"And yet you will."

She said it with certainty. Every time she lost something, which was often, Gilda would always make her say, "When I find it," as if the certainty would make it happen.

"I hope so."

He ran his hand through the loose strands of her hair, pulling them apart, the pleasure of his touch shooting down to her toes.

She looked back down at his chest, using the markings as an excuse to explore his chest. Although she'd had little occasion to see other men in such a state, Marian did not believe for a moment most looked quite like this underneath their tunics.

She traced the flames that started just above his waistline and licked up, toward his stomach. The words *Soul Survivor* spread across the entire length of his stomach.

"And this one?"

"That one—"

A knock on the door interrupted him. "Breakin' our fast, brother."

She recognized the voice as Alban's.

"See you in a few," Greyson called out.

Marian smiled. "We'll be right along," she corrected.

"If we were staying here, I might try harder to assimilate. But we're not. So it's 'see you in a few.'" His free hand grasped hers. "Best you remember it," he teased in an accent that sounded very little like his clansmen.

"Perhaps you are right not to try."

The hand that had been playing with her hair now grabbed it instead. Pulling her head toward him, Greyson pressed his lips to hers without warning. His kiss reminded her of what he'd made her feel the night before, as if she'd needed the reminder.

She wanted that again.

When he pulled her on top of him, Marian groaned against his mouth. His hips circled as she pressed down harder, knowing instinctively what waited for her, maybe just out of reach.

"Keep it up," he said, his voice tickling her ear, "and we'll be more than husband and wife in name only."

"I know little," she responded, neither moving against him nor attempting to get up, "of the ways between men and women, but I do know this does not necessarily lead to marriage."

Greyson stopped moving.

"In your time, it does. No? I didn't think casual sex was a thing here, at least among nobles."

"Casual sex?" She had so much to learn.

"Making love outside of marriage."

"No," she said hesitantly. "'Tis not 'a thing,' as you say."

Greyson flipped them around so suddenly, pinning her under him, the bed creaked from their weight.

"If you had any idea how much I want you . . ."

If she hadn't known before, Marian was pretty sure she did now. He looked at her the way no man ever had before.

"Greyson . . ."

She wanted him to know, to understand. He was not merely a way out of her marriage with Duncan. This bond between them was so much more.

"Grey," he said, peering into her eyes. He leaned down to kiss her, slowly this time, then sprang from the bed. His back, covered with the same type of tattoos as his front, though not so covered she couldn't see his skin beneath.

Hard, muscled . . . were all men as such in his time?

"My family calls me Grey."

She would not misconstrue his words to mean more than they did. He meant only that she was now a familiar.

"Grey," she said, trying it out. The sound he made in response made her wish they could stay here, in this room, for the rest of the day.

Maybe forever.

"I quite like it."

I quite like you.

"Shall we join the others?"

He leaned down to pick up the linen shirt he must have discarded in the night.

"Aye, Maid Marian, we shall."

She laughed at his jest, hope blooming inside her. They would find his family and make their way back through time. It was only a matter of when. Because the alternative was one she refused to consider.

"Greetings. Please, come this way."

The small, kindly woman ushered them into what looked more like a castle than a manor. Greyson hadn't liked being separated from Marian, but she had been whisked away the moment they rode through the gates.

Marian had not batted an eye when a man who identified himself as the steward ushered her through the entranceway toward a young girl. Why she needed rest while they were brought to the hall for food, he could only imagine. On one memorable occasion from his youth, one of his father's business contacts had literally shoved his mother aside so he could speak with his father in private. The insult had pissed his father off enough for him to sever a very lucrative connection.

The midday meal was already underway when they entered the hall, and immediately an entire table of men turned to look at them. No, not look. Grimace was a better word.

"I thought you said this was a safe place?" he whispered to Alban, stopping them both.

"Balliol allies. They know us as supporters of Bruce."

They should have waited for Ross.

Greyson had argued against making themselves known here, but the others had insisted Marian would be safe. By now he understood that the situation they'd stumbled into was not a simple one. A few of his many long talks with Marian had veered into politics.

The Guardians may have officially recognized the baby Margaret as heir to the throne of Scotland, but that didn't stop others from positioning themselves to make a claim if necessary, which it would turn out to be.

His mother's clan, supporters of Robert the Bruce. Some said he was too old to ever see the Crown, but that didn't stop him from putting in his bid.

His current nemesis, John Balliol, seemed like he had a fair claim being the descendant of David I. Though what the hell did Greyson know?

And then there was John Comyn, the underdog from what Greyson could tell.

Finally, King Edward of England. From what Marian had

told him, the Bruce's actions against Balliol had been intended as a signal to Edward—a not-so-subtle hint that he was more powerful than any of the other claimants. And perhaps Edward already knew that, which was why he'd roped Greyson's mom into Irvine's plot.

His mother's clan was backing the winning horse, but that wouldn't be for years to come. In the meantime, King Edward would wreak havoc on Scotland. He knew that from discussions he'd overheard between his mom and Rhys. Plus, he'd seen *Braveheart*. It seemed to him like a good time to find his family and get the hell out of Dodge. Somehow, though, they'd need to warn the others of the dangers they faced as he'd warned Marian, whose rightful concern still bothered him.

Hell, they faced life-and-death situations here on an almost daily basis.

Thankfully, they hadn't been threatened or bothered by anyone since leaving Quinting. That might be about to change.

"So that means they could have reason to share Marian's location with the Earl of Fife. If the topic were to arise."

"They will nae do it."

And here he'd thought New Orleans politics were confusing.

"And why is that?"

As the rest of their party sat two tables away from the men in question, he and Alban remained alongside a wall at the entrance to the hall. Much, much smaller than Quinting Castle, Hallstead hardly fit Greyson's newly formed impression of a manor.

"See the one glaring at Brodie?" Alban asked.

Greyson tried to not be obvious as he glanced over.

"Yeah?"

"His wife is Brodie's older sister."

"What? How the hell is that possible?"

"You may avoid asking either of them. Neither are happy

about the arrangement, about the new allegiances it requires. But it was a love match."

He said it as if the fact was supposed to mean something.

"And?"

By now Alban knew something was very wrong about Greyson. But Ross had introduced him as a relative, and the men had all accepted him as such. The look Alban gave him now, though, held all of the suspicion with which Greyson looked at every potential new business partner.

Greyson ignored it.

"None would have made such a match for any other reason. 'Tis the reason marrying for love should be outlawed."

Greyson started to laugh until he realized Alban was deadly serious.

"So they don't like each other," he said, trying to cover up his gaff. "How does that make Marian safe?"

Alban shook his head as if Greyson were beyond help. Not bothering to answer, he nudged him toward the trestle tables.

Was it that outrageous of a question?

Why were Alban and the others so skittish in Kenfern but confident now, in a manor hosting guests they considered enemies? Because, despite the look of venom Balliol's men still gave them, they felt comfortable enough to stride right inside as if they owned the place.

A bond of marriage. An unwanted one, but a bond nevertheless.

Brodie and his brother-in law. Two men who did nothing more than grunt at each other in passing. But Alban thought their dubious connection enough to protect all of them.

As he sat, he felt the same niggling doubt that had always pricked at him just before he made a big decision at work—a feeling he'd come to recognize, and trust, after years of negotiations and countless instances of getting burned.

He had much to learn about how to navigate this world.

More than he wanted to master. With luck, Ross would get here soon and they could make their way to Perthshire, find his mom and Rhys, and get the hell out of here before he had to learn much more.

2 0

———

"Ye're not keepin' her."

Ross was angry.

Really, really, really angry. Like his two least favorite McCaim Shipping board of directors tossed in a blender and stuffed into a thirteenth-century plaid kind of angry.

Greyson couldn't believe he'd been glad to learn his uncle had returned. A servant had found him in Hallstead's expansive gardens, and he'd immediately hurried back to the hall to see Ross. A servant had led him to this small covered area between the main keep and the kitchens. At least the smell of baking bread and smoke coming from open windows seemed to indicate as much.

If only he could go back to the gardens, where he and Marian had found a rare minute of privacy prior to the interruption.

In the past week, they'd been alone together precisely three times. On none of the three occasions had they shared anything more than a kiss so chaste not even a nun would object. She had a private bedchamber, but he'd been sleeping in the stables with the other men. The last time he'd seen a hayloft had been many years earlier, and he certainly hadn't slept there. He wasn't doing much sleeping there now, truth be told. But judging from the general reaction to Marian traveling with them sans an escort, one that would give even an old-fashioned schoolmarm a run for their money, he'd known better than to try sneaking into her bedroom.

Greyson tried again.

"I'm not a pimp," he said, fully aware his uncle would have no idea what that meant. "And I don't 'keep' women. Marian is free to do as she pleases. And it just so happens it pleases her to stay with us for the moment."

"Nay, lad, she is not. Your peculiar notions of women are out of place here."

My peculiar notions of women.

"Uncle, please listen." Greyson hoped the reminder of their familial tie might calm him down a bit. "I'd planned to escort her, as you commanded," he said, reassuring his uncle that he remembered who was in charge, "but she was worried. The poor woman thinks she'll be blamed for the delay. Instead of mourning the loss of her men, she's forced to consider the feelings of some asshole who apparently no one thinks is worthy of cleaning a toilet never mind marrying someone like Marian."

"Asshole? Toilet? Ye're off yer head, boy." Ross appeared slightly less red than he had a few minutes ago, but no less pissed.

"Arse," he corrected. "Privy."

"I shouldae explained better, but I'm not accustomed to my orders being questioned. By my own nephew, no less."

Greyson could keep Ross here all day with a list of everything that he wanted or needed an explanation for, but he smartly remained silent. As he often did with the only other two men he'd back down from. Ross reminded him so much of both Dad and Rhys.

Ross ran a hand through his hair, hiding his exasperation a little better this time.

"I've barely tempered Bruce, who nearly undid the good work of our envoy to King Edward's regent. His ambitions and hatred of Balliol threaten our stability, but thankfully he listened to reason. And now you must do the same."

Greyson appreciated the effort his uncle was making to explain the situation. He could tell temperance was unnatural for him. But it would do the man no good. He would not forsake Marian.

"Lady Marian is nae just any woman. She is the daughter of an earl who has the ear of the king. One who deemed an alliance with the Earl of Fife worthy of his daughter. I'll remind you, the earl is one of the Guardians. The one most supportive of Bruce's claim. When they discover who was responsible for failing to deliver the lady to her betrothed, it will not bode well for relations between our clan and the Bruce."

He didn't mince words at least.

"You must take her to her betrothed."

He didn't hesitate. "I will not."

Ross growled. "Then I will do it."

"No, you will not."

No one had ever accused Greyson of being a shrinking flower.

Ross's eyes widened at the insubordination, but before he could fly into a rage, Greyson hastened to speak. "The Maid of Norway will not rule Scotland. Neither will Balliol or Bruce. After a bloody intervention by the English king that we'll call the Scottish Wars of Independence, Bruce's grandson will rule. But the cost will be high, and I fear for our clan."

That he said *our clan* was likely the only reason Ross hadn't gone off on him yet. But it was true. These were his mothers' relatives, and his, and Greyson felt nearly as responsible for them as he did his mother and brother.

"I didn't plan to tell you so bluntly, but that's the truth of it. In the meantime, Marian doesn't need to suffer unnecessarily for what will amount to a nonfactor in a much greater war."

Ross, or the Viking, as he'd once thought of him, crossed his big hulking arms. Sometimes he wondered how this man could possibly be his mother's brother, but one look at his determined eyes was all the reminder he needed.

"Will you tell that to both the earls, then? The marriage will not take place because"—he lowered his voice even though they were hidden—"you're from the future, have seen the outcome, and their alliance matters not? Will you explain the situation to Bruce when he finds out Clan MacKinnish was responsible for angering his closest ally, the only one of the Guardians who supports his claim to the throne?"

"A throne now promised to the Maid of Norway."

Ross's brows furrowed.

"The baby Margaret," he clarified.

"None, not even the Guardians who passed their message through me to England, believe she will rule. Much can happen between now and when she comes of age."

Greyson struggled to remember why, precisely, she did not take the throne. He really should have paid better attention in history class, or at least to his mother's tales. But that had been her thing with Rhys.

"So you position yourselves in the meantime?"

"Aye. And your clan's position is by Bruce's side. You will take her back. Or I will do it."

"No one is taking Marian anywhere," he countered.

Ross had apparently had enough of their conversation. "*Lady Marian.*"

He grunted and walked away, leaving Greyson to consider his next move.

Bottom line: he didn't give a shit about customs or alliances or the fact that he was imposing his very twenty-first century ideals on a time and place he had no right to reside in. What mattered was Marian's free will. And finding his mother and brother. He'd prefer to do it with Ross, but if his uncle proved stubborn, then they would have to part ways. How hard could it be to find Perthshire anyway?

"We're lost."

She should have gone with the MacKinnishes.

When Ross had come to her, telling her to prepare her things for the journey to her betrothed, she had done something foolish. Something that could very well cost both her and Grey their lives.

She'd gone to Grey instead, and he'd taken her away. They'd ridden off toward Perthshire alone, just the two of them. A horrible mistake given their current situation.

"We should go back," she said, repeating the words she'd already said several times that afternoon.

"If Perthshire is north, as you say, we are not lost. We just haven't arrived yet."

"Nor will we arrive if that wheel is any indication."

Nodding to the broken, abandoned wooden wheel by the side of the road as they rode past it, Marian waited for Grey's reaction. They'd already ridden by that same wheel earlier in the day, but he shook off her concern.

"I could tell we veered too far east for a time. But we're fine now."

"Despite the fact that we've just ridden in a circle?"

"Aye."

She laughed despite the very real possibility they would die on this road before ever reaching Perthshire. Marian had tried to tell Grey as much when he'd suggested his reckless plan. But he'd refused to listen to reason. If they stayed, he'd insisted, Marian would find herself on horseback before day's end, on her way once again to Duncan.

But perhaps that would have been the wiser course. On the ride north, Grey had told her everything Ross had said to him. While she knew her father desperately wanted the alliance with the Earl of Fife, she had not realized that same earl was Bruce's strongest ally among the Guardians. The one who would, when and if the time came, back Bruce in a claim for the Scottish crown.

By agreeing to stay with Grey, she'd put his clan in real danger of incurring Bruce's wrath. And if Irvine's friend was to be believed, King Edward had been complicit in Alexander's murder, which made him their enemy too. He'd mentioned a baron, too, but had named no names.

Which was why she'd spent the day attempting to convince Grey to return to Hallstead Manor. But he refused to waver, insisting all would be well, and that his *Boy Scout skills*, whatever that meant, would eventually steer them in the right direction. And perhaps he wasn't wrong. As night began to fall, a light appeared in the distance.

Grey squinted at the buildings they approached. "An inn? In the middle of nowhere? Is that normal?"

Marian could see the truth of his words. It was indeed an inn, though by the size of it, finding available rooms might prove tricky. She sincerely hoped there was space. Grey had not seemed concerned by the possibility of *making camp*, as he called it, but she was still unsure what his time *backpacking and staying in plenty of lean-tos* meant, exactly. The arrangement was simple, just two buildings in a partial clearing not far from the road. A bubbling sound indicated the inn was perched just along a stream, maybe a river. Earlier that day they'd started following one, the reason Grey was so confident in the direction they traveled. Was this that same river?

As they got closer, there was just enough light for them to see the sign hanging from the rafters of the straw-topped inn: an image of a cock and a crow.

"The Cock and Crow," Grey said with a smile. "God, I love it. Y'all have the best names. If we ever get back, *when* we get back, I'm opening a tavern in the Quarter with one of these names on it."

"Y'all?"

She'd heard him say it more than once, and could understand the meaning easily. But it served as yet another reminder Grey was not from her time. "'Tis a common phrase in your century?"

As they dismounted and made their way to the stable, Grey explained that it was. Of sorts.

"We have dialects, just as you do here, even within my country."

"The United States of America?"

Grey smiled again, that lazy yet confident smile that reminded her of the first day they'd met.

"You got it. And I'm from . . ."

"Louisiana"—she made a face—"named after a future king of France."

"The relations between your two countries don't improve much, by the way," Grey said, lowering his voice as they approached. "English wars with France will last into the twentieth century."

Marian did not doubt it.

"THE REINS, MY LADY?"

A stableboy emerged from the dark to take the reins from Marian, reminding Greyson to be careful of what he said. Talking about events that would happen hundreds of years from now was a sure way to see them burned at the stake. If they truly did that sort of thing in this era.

He would have to ask Marian about that.

"Many thanks." She smiled at the boy, who looked as if he'd not bathed in many days. He marveled, once again, at how little she acted like the stuffy English noblewoman he might expect. To be fair, Greyson always took it as a compliment when he was told he acted nothing like a billionaire golden boy. He had his parents to thank for that.

And now he knew why.

His mother's clan was clearly influential, her father a laird, but there was a grittiness to this time, even among the elite, that no twenty-first century hardships could match.

After handing over the horses, they made their way to the front of the small inn. Greyson took a deep breath before opening the front door. From the first kick his uncle had given him the day he'd come through, Greyson had come to expect shit and more shit in each new situation they encountered.

This time, he was pleasantly surprised.

"It's a friggin' scene from *Lord of the Rings*," he muttered.

Marian leveled him a sharp glare, and he coughed to cover his slip.

Small but cozy. Like if a neighborhood bar met a quaint bed-and-breakfast. It reminded him of an old-time tavern he'd visited once in Gettysburg. Dark but with enough light to see easily thanks to an open fire in the middle of the room, surrounded by stones. It seemed chimneys were reserved for the manors and castles, the vent in the roof above them the only way for the fire's smoke to escape. Surprisingly, it wasn't smoky, and the fire's location lent a certain coziness to the space.

He loved it.

Reaching into one of the two bags they'd used to transport as much coin as possible from Marian's dowry trunk, he tossed a coin to the innkeeper, who caught it easily. He was only one of four people in the whole place.

"Tankard of ale, a meal and a room?"

Without waiting for a response, he guided them to a small table near the edge of the room.

"You've quickly become accustomed to our ways," Marian said, sitting across from him.

"Acclimate or die," he responded, wishing it were some twisted hyperbole but dreading the truth of those words.

"I feared we may have to answer questions." Her gaze shifted to two men playing chess by the fire. "Reivers?" she whispered.

"You're asking me?"

He studied their padded gambesons, as Ross had called them, remembering seeing a hobbler, another word he'd learned from Ross, just inside the stable as they walked by.

"Most likely," he agreed. "And him?"

Another man sat alone, looking straight at them. Unlike the others, he was dressed well. A knight, probably English by the looks of him.

Greyson knew a challenge when he saw one. He waited for the other man to break eye contact. When he finally looked back at Marian, she was shaking her head softly.

"You've a strange way about you," she said.

"Why, thanks," he said.

The innkeeper brought them two bowls of stew, and Greyson didn't hesitate to dig in. His appetite hadn't diminished since coming through time, but his weight probably had.

She didn't elaborate as they ate mostly in silence. A comfortable silence in a comfortable room that could almost make him forget the shitstorm they were in at the moment.

He could tell Marian was uneasy about her role in all of it. She'd asked to go back no less than fifty times that day. But he wasn't going to let that happen. If they went back to Hallstead, he knew without a doubt Ross wouldn't hesitate to whisk Marian away.

"I've been thinking," he said quietly between bites, "it must not have been a coincidence that I came back to exactly this time and literally dropped at my uncle's feet."

"You said your aunt was given that cross by the fae?"

"Mmm-hmmm."

"And that you and your brother only came through after your brother learned one of the words of the chant had been incorrect."

His mouth full of stew, Greyson nodded.

"We know little about moving through time," she said, speaking so softly her words were barely audible, "other than 'tis possible. Do you think the cross is necessary?"

"It must be."

"Then . . ." She swallowed, but he already knew what Marian was going to say. "How are we to get back?"

Greyson shrugged his shoulder. "My aunt must have found another one to pull my mother back."

But she didn't look relieved. Her brow furrowed. "And being dropped at your uncle's feet. You think that was meant to happen? That you were supposed to meet Ross?"

Finished eating, Greyson wiped his mouth and sat back, mug in hand. "It's a big country. I could have ended up anywhere. Somehow, the enchantment, or whatever it is, knows things. You could say it was chance my mother dropped in the French Quarter, or you could say it happened by design. Either way, it was lucky she ended up in a place with a history of cultures blending and clashing, where a woman in medieval garb would hardly attract notice."

He took a swig of ale, accustomed to the maltier, sweeter taste now. "Which makes me wonder if my mother will actually be in Perthshire, if she did come through, or some other place. But I don't know where because I don't know why she needed to come back."

He waited for Marian's reaction.

"You believe if your brothers come through, they will fall into the right places as well?"

Much to Ian's dismay, Greyson was an eternal optimist. So yes, he believed that.

"Maybe it's wishful thinking," he said, "but the more I think about it, aye, I do believe it."

Marian's eyes softened as she smiled.

"And that your mother came back to the very place she needed to be as well?"

He held her gaze and nodded once, hoping she would carry the line of reasoning a step further, just like he had. Something sparked in her eyes, and he leaned forward, reaching his hand across the table. She took it, more hesitantly than he would have liked.

"You think we were meant to meet?"

If Greyson wasn't meant to be sitting here with this strong, beautiful woman, surrounded by the warmth of a raging fire in a room more pleasant than it had any right to be given its remote location, then he was a damn fool for believing it.

But he'd learned to trust his instincts, and he was following their lead now.

Why, then, did the revelation seem to distress Marian? He was sure she cared for him too, but something held her back.

"What is it?"

Still holding his hand, Marian took a drink with the other,

the cloud of uncertainty that had passed over her features already gone.

"I believe—"

Marian's words were cut off when the door unceremoniously slammed open, and the first pleasant evening he'd had in a long while came to an abrupt end.

"Who is it?" Marian asked from the other side of her door, just to be certain. She'd been waiting for Grey. When she'd excused herself from the hall so he could speak to his uncle, who had found them, he'd whispered to her, "I will come to you."

"Greyson." She opened the door before he finished. Quickly stepping inside, Grey closed it behind him and hesitated just briefly before pulling her into his arms. Marian went to him willingly.

At first, she thought she could be content to simply lay her head on his chest, to breathe in the unique scent that was Greyson McCaim. But after just a few moments of listening to the rapid beating of his heart beneath her ear, she wanted more.

She wanted to know his talk with Ross had gone well. That his uncle had agreed she should stay with him and that they would continue to Perthshire on the morn.

But when she pulled away from his chest, she knew immediately that had not been the outcome. There was little light in this small room, but enough for her to see his tortured eyes. Standing on her toes, Marian kissed him, initiating for the first time.

She took what she wanted, exactly as Grey had promised that she could. The sense of freedom was almost as glorious as the feel of his lips on hers. The kiss quickly consumed them both, but Marian's worries wouldn't leave her. What had Ross said to him? Did he know Grey was with her now?

Marian pushed the thoughts aside, letting herself be in this very real moment. He might not be from her time, but Grey was flesh and blood, in her bedchamber, and if she were being honest, she'd fallen in love with him.

And although Marian had not known the love of a man before, she thought perhaps this might be how it felt.

Pushing against his chest ever so slightly, Marian sighed at the look on his face. Probably the same look she wore on her own.

Desperation. Admiration.

Love.

"Tell me what happened."

If she'd wanted to quench the spark that had ignited between them, her question had been effective. Running a hand through his hair, Grey pulled away and sat on the bed. Marian wanted to join him.

She really, really wanted to join him.

But she didn't. Instead, she sat on the wooden chair, remembering the last time they'd sat this way—one on the bed, one on the chair. How was it possible she'd come to be here, in this small room at the Cock and Crow in quite literally the middle of Scotland, with a man who had somehow come through time?

He's right. The enchantment, or whatever it is, knows things.

"He was not very pleased."

She knew him well enough to sense he was holding back.

"Where is your uncle now?"

"In the hall with the others. He'll likely not be pleased to discover that I've gone missing." Grey's chin lifted. "Ross reminds me of my father in many ways. How he was before Mom disappeared."

When he looked at her, the pain of having left his father was evident. Grey's family was never far from his thoughts. As it should be. As she'd always wished it would be for her.

It seemed she would need to pull the information from him.

"What did your uncle say?"

Grey closed his eyes, the tic in his jaw more prominent now than she'd ever seen it before. Marian understood the battle raging inside of him, for the same battle was underway inside her.

"That if we do not bring you to Duncan, his father will blame Clan MacKinnish. Rightfully so, I suppose, but the repercussions . . . Ross believes our relations with Bruce will suffer."

"Does he believe the Earl of Fife could pull his support of Bruce in retaliation?"

Marian held her breath, waiting for the answer.

"He believes it's inevitable."

Marian wanted to hang her head, but showing Grey her disappointment would not do. He would attempt to comfort her. Mayhap even guess her intentions.

And she could not let him know what she was thinking.

"What will you do?" she asked.

"Nothing. We will continue to Perthshire and find my mother and brother."

"And leave what in your wake?"

Grey stood, coming to her. "I need to prove to my uncle that Clan MacKinnish shouldn't get involved in a fight that is not theirs. They will all likely die for an outcome that cannot be changed. All the posturing in the world isn't going to make Bruce or Balliol king. Not yet."

Marian was not so sure of that. If Grey and his brothers had been brought back for a reason, perhaps this was the reason.

"But what if we could change things? What if Bruce is made

aware of Edward's involvement?" she asked. "Of his aspirations for the Crown of Scotland? If Alexander was killed on his orders, Bruce needs to know."

She took Greyson's hand and stood.

"A risky proposition, Marian. We have no way of knowing if the future can be changed. There are dozens of books and movies about people trying to do just that, and while those stories are fiction, there's one common theme: it's a dangerous thing, to try to change the inevitable."

Once she would have needed to ask him to explain his strange words, but Grey had told her of movies. And pictures. And planes. She believed all of it. Believed him.

But if his knowledge of the future could not help him, then she knew of only one thing that could . . .

It would do them no good if they angered her father, the Earl of Fife, and Bruce. Perhaps King Edward's success was inevitable, but that didn't mean they couldn't start another war in the meantime.

"Neither of us knows much about how your being here will affect the future. Or if it can, indeed, be altered." She stopped, knowing her next argument would be wasted on him. "Your uncle will be looking for you," she said instead, her heart heavy.

"Aye," he teased, kissing her. And when she kissed him back, it was with the knowledge that this would be the last time their lips met. The last time Marian would find herself in the arms of a man she loved, and who loved her.

Neither of them had said the words, but she felt them in the tender way he touched her. Saw them in the way he looked at her. It was a powerful emotion, love, and one she should be blessed to have felt, if only for a short time.

She felt the heaviness of that thought, and unfortunately, he noticed.

Pulling away, he looked into her eyes for much too long. But instead of questioning her, he said, "We *will* make this work."

Marian knew otherwise, but she held her tongue. Often able to see the best in most situations, this particular one tested her like none other.

"I have to go, but tomorrow, on the way to my mother's, we'll talk about the future."

"The future," she mumbled, "sounds like a time I would like very much."

With a final squeeze of her hands, Grey smiled. "You will love it. Although Reikart will be pissed. He's a big fan of the bachelor pad, as he calls it."

She didn't have to ask. Grey could tell she had little idea what that meant.

"Never mind. I'll explain tomorrow," he said. "I'll see you in the morning. Lock the door behind me."

She tried to smile back, but Marian knew it didn't quite reach her eyes. Grey was too distracted to notice. Likely worried about his uncle, he left with a final wink. The door had barely closed before her eyes welled, thinking of that last gesture. Then another vision came to her, that of her maid. How was Gilda faring at Fenwall? Had she heard of their attack? Had her father?

If they did not know yet, word would reach them soon enough. And when she did not arrive in Pittillock, her father would be enraged. She'd only seen him lose his temper once—violently, at that. King Edward had censured him for forming an alliance with the Bishop of Glasgow. While it was not unusual for English border lords to ally with their Scottish neighbors, as they did with the Earl of Fife, that particular connection had apparently not been approved by their sovereign. The king's regent had paid them a visit the year before to condemn the alliance. She'd happened upon her father that same night, raging in his solar. The coin he'd promised Robert Wishart, the bishop, was rescinded, which was precisely when talk of her betrothal had begun.

The connection had never occurred to her before, but perhaps that meant Edward wished for her to marry Duncan. Why?

It mattered not. As Grey had said, it was too dangerous to meddle with events that had not yet happened, the effect unknown. And it was much too dangerous for Clan MacKinnish to harbor someone who might tear apart their own alliances.

After all, someday, according to Grey, the Bruce family would be one of kings.

With any luck, the McCaim family would find themselves safely back at home, in New Orleans, free from the turmoil of this time.

Of her time.

2 3

"WHAT THE FUCK do you mean, 'They're gone'?"

Greyson didn't care about being careful. He didn't give a shit if anyone thought his language peculiar. The only thing he cared about at the moment was the two words Brodie had just uttered.

When he woke up before sunrise to a serving girl's hushed pleas for his uncle to follow her, Greyson, like the others, had attempted to join him. But his uncle had waved them off, assuring the men that it was a small matter and none of them were needed. Telling them they could return to sleep.

The piercing sound of a rooster, no less annoying in this century than his own, had awoken Greyson some time later. Brodie had still been in the room, but the others were gone. Gone, he'd assumed, to prepare for their departure.

But Greyson had stumbled out to the stables to check for Marian's trunk—part of his ritual given his worry someone would steal her money—only to find the cart horse was gone. Indeed, all of the horses were gone.

He'd hurried out of the stables, hoping to find the mounts waiting outside. But they weren't there either.

"Brodie?" he'd shouted as the other man walked out toward him. "Where are the men?"

The other man had at least possessed the grace to look guilty.

"They're gone."

After flinging his expletive-laden question at Brodie, Greyson tore into the inn, through the main room and up the creaky stairs. There were just four doors, one of which was . . . he tossed it open to find exactly what he'd been expecting.

Nothing.

Marian's bedchamber was empty, no sign of her anywhere. Greyson looked at the chair she'd sat in the night before, his heart lurching.

She'd known.

Marian had known it would be their last night together. That look she'd given him, the one he'd tried to discern before nearly telling her . . .

God dammit. Why hadn't he just said the words? Would it have been so difficult to say *I love you*? Maybe it would have made a difference. Maybe she would have stayed.

Sitting on the bed, Greyson buried his face in his hands. She was gone, and Ross had taken her.

Traitor.

Just fucking great.

Dad was in the hospital, in a coma. Rhys and Mom were God knew where. Reikart and Ian were, at best, mourning the loss of nearly every friggin' family member except each other. And now she was gone.

The enormity of it sank into his chest, the dull pain a familiar one at this point, but no more welcome than it had been when his mother had first gone missing. He'd been so eager to bring Marian back. Show her everything that had come to pass in seven hundred years. Introduce her to his family after they reunited Mom and Dad. The doctor had said he could still recover, and Greyson had no doubt his mother's voice was the one thing that would pull his father back to them.

"Greyson?"

He didn't want to talk. Not to Brodie, not to anyone.

But he wasn't sure the Viking's minion would appreciate being told to fuck off. He did have one question, though.

"How did they manage it?"

Brodie knew exactly what he was talking about. His sheepish shrug was as delicate as the Scots warrior was likely to get.

"I've always slept like the dead"—he looked up to the rafters—"but all of them, and the horses too?"

He was talking more to himself, but Brodie answered.

"They brought the cart outside the stable last eve." Brodie sat in the chair not long ago occupied by Marian. A much less pleasant sight. "So as not to wake you."

Greyson thought back to the serving girl who'd awoken his uncle.

"She sent a maid to Ross."

"Aye."

"Who was all too happy to take her away from under my nose."

Brodie's quizzical look would have to go unanswered. He was in no mood to explain his *odd sayings* at the moment.

He sprang from the bed. If Ross, or Marian for that matter, thought he would sit here and twiddle his thumbs while she sacrificed herself for the good of his clan, both of them were in for a rude awakening.

"I need a horse," he muttered, leaving the empty chamber.

"You'll find none here," Brodie said, his brogue thick, behind him. "The other visitors have all left, and it could be days before the Cock and Crow receives new ones."

"Then somewhere else. Another inn. A castle. Somewhere . . ."

The lack of a response disturbed him. Greyson turned in the dimly lit corridor, the only light from the stairwell ahead.

"How far exactly?"

Brodie shrugged. "Brentford Abbey is just north."

"Just?"

He didn't like the look on the other man's face.

"Walking, you could get there"—he shrugged—"in two or three days' time."

Two or three days. And if he could secure a horse at this abbey, he would still have to somehow catch up with them. Before they reached the Earl of Fife. He'd travel faster alone, without a cart horse, but still . . .

"Bollocks, Greyson, you are not planning to follow them?"

He would have liked to say, I didn't come through time, find an uncle I didn't know I had and a woman I didn't know I needed to let one deliver the other to a lifetime of misery. But he didn't. Instead, he asked his clansman a question.

"Damned right I am. Now are you coming with me or nae?"

24

IF SHE HAD THOUGHT LEAVING her home to journey north to a man she did not wish to marry was awful, this day was much, much worse. Not only would she be delivered to Duncan soon, but she went to him knowing what it meant to love. And be loved.

Knowing the kindling of desire and the feel of a kiss that left her wanting more.

Knowing a man existed who thought her capable and strong when Marian had seen herself as neither for so long.

That it was the right thing to do mattered little. Nor did it matter that Ross and the others agreed with her. Of course they would, for she did it for the good of their clan. For Greyson. But that did not make Marian feel any better.

When she'd asked the serving girl to fetch Ross, a part of her had hoped he would say, *Nay, you've no need to do this.* It would have forced her into a quandary, of course, but maybe she'd not be sitting astride her horse, the trunk of gold that was her entire worth to her father bouncing up and down in front of her.

Marian could not stop staring at that gilded trunk, thinking of what lay inside. With every moment that passed, she hated it more and more. Grey had mentioned a saying he loved, one he'd clung to after his mother's disappearance. All day she'd tried to convince herself to *be happy that it happened rather than sad that it was over*, but she simply could not do it.

This would all have been so much easier if she'd never met him.

"Lady Marian, we'd not planned to stop before the abbey. Unless you must do so?"

Ross had ridden up to her, but it took Marian a few moments for his words to penetrate. They would be staying at St. Aberdeen this eve. At this pace, they would reach Duncan's estate in two days' time.

"There is no need to stop for me," she said. Marian had become accustomed to drinking just a bit less on long-riding days, making the need to stop less pressing.

She'd become accustomed to many new things since leaving Fenwall, some she now wished to forget.

"If there were a way to avoid this, we would do it easily, lass."

His expression was pained, and Marian did not doubt the truth of his words. Ross had been kind to her from the start and had expressed regret at agreeing with the choice she'd made, to leave Greyson.

He slowed, so Marian did the same. Before long, the cart horse rode well ahead of them.

"He told you," Ross said.

It was not a question, so Marian didn't feel the need to respond. She and Ross had never spoken about Grey's unique position.

"My sister, Grace, his aunt . . . for as far back as I can remember, the lass has gotten herself into trouble. Consorting with fae . . ." He tsked, clearly displeased. "We warned her. Eventually, my father would say, someone was bound to notice her abilities. But this—" Ross shook his head. "'Tis hard to believe, but the truth of it was impossible to ignore. My other sister, Shona, Greyson's mother—their resemblance is unmistakable."

"Do you believe she is here? Shona? That she's come back?"

The wind picked up around them, rain certainly threatening.

"It seems likely, aye. Irvine may be dead, but I fear she is in danger still. His companion implicated your English king and a baron he did not name. 'Tis a tangle we've yet to fully untie."

Your English king.

But he wasn't hers any longer. Marian would be married to a Scot, the young babe across the sea in Norway her sovereign now. Truly it did not matter. She'd belonged nowhere for so long . . .

"I am sorry for it, lass."

Marian looked up at the fearsome face of a man who had protected her, who was clearly torn about the role he played now . . . she felt poorly for him. No one should be forced to make such a choice.

"'Tis not your fault. I am the daughter of the Earl of Fenwall. My duty has always been clear." Marian held her chin high despite knowing she rode toward a fate she hated—one she would have done anything to escape. "I hope the son is better than the father. It appears we are on the same side, at least. From what Grey said, it seems the Bruce family will emerge victorious in the end."

Ross made a sound low in his throat, sounding almost like a growl. "After what Greyson claims to be a long and bloody war."

"Claims? Do you not believe him?"

Ross didn't answer right away, but Marian understood anyway. Even as she'd come to believe Grey, some of his claims were so far-fetched her mind could not fully grasp the impact of them.

Finally, he said, "If the chance presents itself, I believe Edward will indeed strip Scotland for his gain. Men such as him care for power and gold, and not much else."

Marian sighed.

Power and gold. She agreed but would add land as well. For her father, it seemed just as important, although she suspected power had figured more into his decision to marry her off. Once again, she thought about the visit the king's regent had paid him last year, and how talk of the engagement had come soon afterward.

Marian pulled back the reins, slowing to a stop as she spotted the cart horse just edging its way over a ridge in front of them.

"What do you suppose my father gains in an alliance with the Earl of Fife? Would he not have done better to marry me to an English noble?"

"Like many of the border lords, his allegiance is not always aligned to country first," Ross said, having stopped with her. "What is it, lass?"

"Bruce attacked Balliol land to send a message to King Edward."

Ross made a face of disgust. "Aye."

"The Earl of Fife is the one Guardian loyal to the Bruce family."

She thought aloud, more for her own benefit than for Ross's. Her thoughts, a tumbling mess, began to run together as the wind picked up. She knew there was a connection but could not yet put it together.

"Did you know my father is a third cousin to Edward?" she asked suddenly, aware Ross had not known. She did not say it to brag. Marian held little love for a man with a reputation such as King Edward's, sovereign or nay.

"I did not."

The king and her father were steadfast allies and would have the very same goals. But what goals were those?

"Rain is coming, my lady. We should be on our way."

Ross had hardly finished speaking when the first drops fell,

Marian unable to finish her thoughts. But thankfully, it did not appear they would be making their way to the abbey after all. When they climbed the ridge, she could see the rest of their party heading toward a small village, likely to take shelter from the rain.

Which suited her well. She urgently needed to continue speaking to Ross.

25

"NEVER ARRIVED?"

Greyson glared at Brodie, which was becoming something of a habit. This was the McCaim glare, named as such by those who worked with him and his brothers. This same glare had always collapsed their business adversaries' best intentions and ensured McCaim Shipping would not be screwed over.

But it had no effect on the Scot, which was how Greyson knew he was telling the truth.

After the hell they'd been through that day, never mind being completely soaked, this was not the news he'd wanted to hear. But there was no way Brodie could fake it so well.

"They were headed here?"

"Aye," Brodie said, "I told ye so already."

He turned to the abbess, the woman whom the nuns had summoned when they'd arrived in the dead of night, asking after a traveling party. Judging by their deference, he assumed she was in charge. She looked the part, and he supposed her title sounded pretty official too.

Shit, he was in a medieval abbey. Sometimes the reality of

this time-traveling thing slapped him in the face like a bad call that saw the Saints booted from the playoffs.

"Ah, my lord. They never arrived," she repeated.

What gave the abbess the impression he was someone to call *my lord*, Greyson had no clue. But he'd have to remember to tell this one to Ian. Maybe he could get the scamp to retire his old nickname in favor of *my lord*.

"How is that possible?" He addressed the question to Brodie, who had no answer but a shrug.

By some massive stroke of luck, the horses hadn't been a problem. Not ten minutes after he'd realized Marian was missing, two riders had arrived at the inn like a gift from the time-traveling gods. And although Greyson normally wouldn't steal from anyone, they hadn't had enough coin to buy the horses outright. Plus, Brodie had said they were reivers—men who thieved for a living. If a person had to steal, ideally it would be from a thief. Still, he didn't want Ian to find out. Man, he'd have a field day with this one.

"Is there another place they might have gone nearby?" he asked, aware they now had an audience. No less than ten nuns stood off to the side, looking at them as if it were a rare occurrence to host a time traveler from New Orleans. Of course, they couldn't know that, and Greyson thought he was doing a pretty good job of fitting in at this point.

"Pellshire, perhaps?"

"Is that the village we passed?"

Brodie nodded.

"Fuck," he muttered before remembering his place. "Pardon me, Sister."

When Brodie looked at him with a mixture of shock and mortification, Greyson realized maybe he wasn't doing such a hot job of pretending to be from the Middle Ages, after all. Cursing was a lot less fun here. And yeah, he had no idea what to call an abbess.

"Lady Mother," Brodie quickly corrected, solving that mystery.

It was easily a three-hour ride back there, and if they were wrong and the others had gone past the abbey, continuing north for some reason . . .

"I am sorry the news causes you distress," the abbess said, looking at him as if he were the devil incarnate. "We will pray for you."

"Tha—" He cleared his throat. "Many thanks, Lady Mother. I apologize for troubling you."

Brodie looked at him with approval this time, almost like Rhys did when he closed a deal for the company. If he couldn't get back to his own time, maybe he could make this medieval thing work.

If he couldn't get back . . .

Greyson had to get back. His father might be dying, and he still had no idea what was happening with his other brothers.

He turned to leave, Brodie following him. They didn't say anything until both were mounted and back on the road.

"To Pellshire?" Greyson said, making it sound like a suggestion even though he had no intention of standing down.

Brodie made the same sound he'd made after Greyson had stolen—borrowed—the horses. He didn't like it, but he'd also not let Greyson roam the countryside alone. Indeed, he followed without trying to dissuade or reason with him. The unwavering commitment to him, to his safety, made him miss his brothers even more.

"Is everyone in Clan MacKinnish related?"

Thankfully, he could hardly see Brodie's face in the moonlight. The guy was probably looking at him like he'd gone crazy. He'd heard his mother talk about her family's history, but he'd assumed she was a genealogy buff, and frankly it hadn't interested him much.

He should have paid more attention.

"Nay, my grandfather was a squire to Laird MacKinnish."

Laird MacKinnish. Greyson's grandfather.

"What is the laird like?"

Brodie navigated them easily despite the dark. These small horses might look a bit strange, but apparently they were accustomed to the terrain.

"Stubborn. Loyal. Not unlike his sons."

Greyson patted his horse as the beast stumbled, quickly righting himself. "Sounds like more than one of my brothers."

"You've brothers, then, aye?"

Shit.

"Three of them." Anticipating the next question, Greyson offered the link Ross had fed to him. "The laird had a brother none speak of who left Perthshire as a young man and lived in London. I am his grandson, though I've not lived in one place long enough to call it home."

Greyson hated lying, but it had to be done. He and Ross had agreed no one but their immediate family should be told about the time traveling.

"A brother . . ."

Greyson could tell Brodie wanted to ask more questions, so he headed them off.

"I've always wanted to come to Scotland," he said, more comfortable for being honest. "I was here only once and for too brief a time. Your country is spectacular."

"Not mine," Brodie offered, "but yours too. Will you stay?"

Wasn't that the question of the century.

"I don't know."

It was the only answer he had, because unfortunately it was brutally true. Greyson had no idea if it was possible to go back, but he would devote all his energy to trying. He needed to find his mother and bring her back to Dad. His dad's life literally depended on it.

They fell into an easy silence, one punctuated by the sounds of the night and by his own heartbeat. He could hear it in his ears as they finally spotted the torches up ahead. The village. Surrounded by fields and encircled with a wooden wall, the few dozen buildings looked like something out of The Sims Medieval. He'd never been a huge gamer, but Greyson knew a bit about medieval town building thanks to his college roommate. Remarkably, the game version was a good facsimile, at least from this distance. The only things missing were Tudor-style homes and a windmill. But as they approached, he could spot a waterwheel at the very edge of the cluster of buildings, a chapel. Maybe only twenty or thirty buildings total.

Was she here? Though the sun hadn't risen yet, judging from the time they'd spent on the road and signs of activity here and there, morning wasn't far away.

What if she's not here? What if she is here but refuses to come with me?

Greyson exchanged a glance with his tenuous ally, fully aware he was Ross's man and not his own. If push came to shove, Greyson would be in this fight alone.

But it was a fight he didn't intend to lose.

A fight for the woman he loved.

26

———

"Are you certain?"

Marian had asked Ross that same question repeatedly the night before. His only response, then and now, was a grunt that could be mistaken, maybe, for an *aye*.

They sat together at one of four trestle tables. The lord and lady of Brennan, the bastille house they now occupied, sat at the front of the small hall.

By the time they'd satisfied the guards stationed just inside the wooden palisade that surrounded the village, Marian and her companions had been soaked, the rain unrelenting for much of the evening. They'd gone to the inn, and would have been content to stay there, but when Lord Brennan learned they were hosting an earl's daughter, he'd invited them to stay. Gracious hosts, they'd provided them with means to dry their clothing, a fine meal, and even a private bedchamber for Marian.

She'd used it to finally have her discussion with Ross, however unusual the arrangement, and they'd stayed awake well into the night.

"Quite certain," he said yet again. Ripping off a hunk of bread and spreading it with freshly churned butter, he took an enormous bite. Judging from their murmurs of delight, Ross and the others clearly approved of the meal. What a treasure they'd found. Marian took a bite of her own buttered bread and could not help but close her eyes in pleasure. Was that honey she tasted?

"Hello, Marian."

Her eyes whipped open. It could not be.

"Wondering how we got here so quickly?"

Marian simply stared as Grey sat down opposite her, nudging his uncle to move down in the process. Ross was apparently as surprised as she felt.

"I have to admit, we got lucky. There are currently two angry reivers, or at least I assume they're pretty angry, who are probably looking to kill me."

"Us," Brodie said from behind her. When he sat down as well, none of the others at the table said a word.

"Fate is funny that way, I guess. Need a horse? One shows up on your doorstep. Or at your inn, in our case."

He was not pleased. Not pleased at all.

Marian swallowed hard.

"We rode through the night but, *surprise*, when we got to Brentford Abbey, you weren't there."

"Greyson, we must talk."

"Aye, we must."

If possible, he was even more upset now than when he'd first sat down. And Ross, bless him, was looking at his nephew as if he'd never seen him before.

"Shall we seek privacy, perhaps?"

But Greyson was already shaking his head. "Oh no," he said, shooting a glance at Ross, "this is for you too."

Their own men weren't the only ones in the hall listening now. Villagers, servants . . . their attention was all on them.

"You'll not be marrying anyone, not unless it's me. I love you, Lady Marian of Fenwall, and as God and my clan are my witnesses, you will not sacrifice yourself for anyone. I will find a way to make this right by Clan MacKinnish, but we will do it together."

No one reacted at their table, but a smattering of applause and the sound of mugs being pounded on tables meant she wasn't the only one in the hall pleased by Greyson's declaration. In fact, despite his anger, Marian couldn't help but smile.

"You love me," she repeated, earning an eye roll from Ross.

"Aye, lass," he said, sounding a little less like the Southerner he'd called himself and more like the grandson of Laird MacKinnish. In fact, Marian could not help but stare at him, the transformation remarkable. He was one of them. Nay, not just one of them—he would be her husband. "I do. Verra much."

Ross snickered.

"Too much?" he asked, the corners of his mouth lifting just slightly.

His uncle nodded and then raised his fist in the air, nodding to the lord and lady. Leaning forward, he lowered his voice for their ears only and said, "We've something to tell you, lad."

He looked pointedly at his nephew, as if to tell him the time for making a scene had ended.

"I realized something," she began, only Greyson and Brodie unaware of what she was about to say. "Why would my father desire the Earl of Fife as an ally?"

Greyson's brows drew together. After his proclamation, that was clearly not what he'd thought she would ask.

"You said you didn't know why," Greyson said.

"And I did not. At least, not before. But my father is quite close to King Edward. And that man, the one who tried to harm"—she nearly said *your mother*—"Ross's sister, his companion alluded to Edward's involvement in Alexander's death."

She could tell Greyson had yet to make the connection.

"And then Bruce attacked Balliol," she whispered, "proving his willingness and ability to fight for Scotland."

"Aye." Greyson shook his head. "But why are you telling me all this?"

"Because," she finished, "I believe my father is helping Edward *appear* to support Bruce by aligning himself with Bruce's allies, such as the Earl of Fife. But in truth, they are really positioning the king to insinuate himself in Scotland's problems of inheritance."

"Problems?" Brodie asked. Marian was prepared for the question as the other men had asked the same. She and Greyson and Ross knew what the future held, but the other men did not. Nor could they.

"Your envoy was only necessary because the babe has such a tenuous hold on the Scottish crown," she said, unable to divulge more. "What if Edward plans to take advantage of that, to assert himself, and do so with the support of the Scottish nobles closest to him?"

"Like Bruce," Greyson finished.

"Aye, like Bruce. Would my father not be rewarded if such were to occur?"

Greyson contemplated her words and then came to the very same conclusion she and Ross had reached the previous night. Marian wasn't sure how they'd not all seen through her father's motives earlier. Part of her was convinced Ross went along with her explanation more out of pity for her and Greyson's situation than anything. But none of that mattered now.

"Your father uses your marriage to Duncan to help Edward secure his position for a future claim?"

Marian cleared her throat, but she could see her warning was unnecessary. Greyson stopped there. Without the benefit of knowing future events, the other men might believe it a tale she'd conjured to get out of her marriage agreement. But she and Greyson and Ross did know the future. And they knew

Edward's plans for Scotland reached far wider than he would admit for a few years to come.

"Your father is despicable," Greyson spat.

Marian did not disagree.

"I leave after breaking my fast," Ross said.

"To?"

"To speak to the Earl of Fife."

Grey clearly did not understand their plan and looked inclined to pounce on his uncle.

"I will not be going with him," she added quickly. "Ross has agreed to negotiate on my behalf. My dowry will be offered as compensation for the broken betrothal, my father's true plans revealed."

"True or nay," Ross finished, " Fife will believe it before I finish. He will take the coin offered, break the marriage agreement, and know the Earl of Fenwall as a man whose only true allegiance is to the King of England. There is, of course, the possibility he could be complicit with Fenwall. I shall ascertain the best way forward with him once there."

Grey's eyes widened.

"You will do that? For Marian?"

"For Marian. For you. For our clan."

This time, Grey's clansmen were the ones who pounded their mugs on the table. *Her* clansmen. They'd accepted her as one of their own.

"And if the earl does not accept your offering?"

That's when she smiled, grateful for the proclamation Grey had made upon entering the hall. She and Ross had an idea about that as well. But she had not wanted to force Grey into it. He'd talked about bringing her back to his time and letting her go free, if she so willed it.

But she did not will it.

Marian wanted only to be with him.

"We did have an idea about that."

Silent this whole time, Alban apparently could hold it in no longer. All of the men knew their tenuous plan.

"You'll be gettin' married this day," Alban broke in with a smile. "The Earl of Fife cannae have her."

She watched Grey's expression carefully. And was pleased by what she saw there.

For the first time since he'd entered the hall, Grey smiled genuinely. He stood, walked around to her side of the table in a few short strides, and fairly lifted her from the bench.

"Now that," he said, kissing her in full view of the others, "is the first piece of good news I've heard in weeks."

THIS WAS NOT the wedding Marian had envisioned when leaving Fenwall.

With Ross anxious to leave, and all of them ready to make their way to Perthshire, arrangements had been made remarkably fast. So fast, indeed, that Marian had not had an opportunity to speak to Grey alone.

Lady Brennan had been more than gracious in helping Marian find a suitable gown. And though they'd just broken their fast, she'd insisted a cake be made in their honor. None seemed to care Marian was an English bride, or that the circumstances surrounding their hasty nuptials were suspicious at best. Even the chaplain had been easily swayed, courtesy of Marian's coin.

But she needed to speak with Grey before the wedding. She had to know this was what he wanted. Lady Brennan's maid had fetched him for her, and now she awaited him in a small, dark chamber at the back of the chapel, her hands trembling.

When the door cracked open, a refreshed groom, hair still wet, entered. He'd shaved too, the change remarkable. Grey looked more like a nobleman now even though he wore the same clothing. He had always stood tall, confidence oozing from him.

But this Grey . . . he'd changed since they first met. She'd noticed earlier, but it was even more pronounced now.

And maybe she had changed too.

"In my time, it's bad luck to see the bride before the ceremony," he said glibly, but then he stopped, his gaze taking her in. He frowned, not the reaction she'd hoped to see. "You look like a noblewoman."

The gown she'd borrowed, one that had belonged to Lady Brennan's daughter, who was now married herself, was indeed lovely. A deep blue velvet lined with gold thread at the sleeves. Marian wore her own gold belt and a necklace she'd taken from her trunks. Lady Brennan had offered her maid's services in arranging her hair atop her head, but she'd insisted on keeping it down, unadorned and untamed.

It was a small act of rebellion on her part. Her father thought it unruly, but Marian had always preferred it that way. It made her feel more like herself.

"You look beautiful."

Marian clenched her hands to stop them from trembling. Grey noticed and took both, squeezing them tightly.

"You're nervous? Marian, Clan MacKinnish is as committed as I am to keeping you safe. You don't need to worry about your father, or your intended, or the Earl of Fife. I promise. We'll protect you. *I* will protect you."

She believed him, but that was not Marian's concern.

"You said once . . ."

Her fears had seemed more reasonable before. Now that he was next to her, holding his hands, she felt safe. He'd always made her feel this way, ever since the day of the attack. Safe and loved.

"You told me you would bring me with you, back through

time." She took a deep breath. "But that I could be free, do as I please."

"And you can. You will," he said with the same conviction he expressed every time they discussed going back to his time.

"That I could be free of you," she clarified.

Grey's eyes widened in understanding.

"Marian, I said that because I wanted true freedom for you. The ability to make your own choices, in all things. If that meant coming to my time but not being with me . . ." He paused. "I also said that I believe fate brought us together. And that I love you. Both of those things are true, Marian. I'd never marry you out of some sense of obligation. If for one reason alone."

"What reason is that?" she asked, already feeling much better.

"When my brother finds out your name, learns we met here, in this time . . ."

He was withholding something from her.

"What is it?"

Grey smiled. "Do you remember what I told you about Robin Hood?"

"Of course. And still you call me Maid Marian at times."

"I failed to mention my brothers, Ian especially, used to call me Robin Hood because of the archery. They still do, actually."

She tried, and failed, not to laugh.

"They call you Robin Hood? And I am . . ."

"Maid Marian"—he made a not very gentlemanly sound —"yeah. So trust me, they'll be busting my ass basically for eternity."

Marian attempted to compose herself.

"If I could have chosen my wife's name, it probably wouldn't have been Marian." He smiled. "But I would choose you no matter what. Any time. Anywhere. So shall we?" He let go of her hands and gestured toward the door.

"Aye," she answered, leading the way. "Robin."

Marian laughed at her own jest all the way to the chapel doors.

- - -

MOM WILL KILL ME.

No fancy procession or reception. Just a woman he'd fallen in love with standing by his side on a cloudy October day in the middle of medieval Scotland.

Not what he, or his mother, had imagined. She loved planning parties and had told them all in no uncertain terms that she'd be unhappy if any of them eloped.

Hopefully this didn't count.

Perhaps it was the happiness of being with Marian, or maybe it was her optimism twining with his, but every day that passed Greyson was more confident that his mother was alive, in this time, and that they would find her. He couldn't wait to introduce Marian to her.

His wife.

Repeating the words of the tired-looking chaplain, Greyson found himself well and truly married, as they would say in this time. If they couldn't get back, he could see himself staying here. He'd adjusted enough to appreciate life without technology. Without distractions.

Unless being attacked on a weekly basis was considered a distraction.

"Do I get to kiss the bride?"

From the chaplain's scowl, it apparently wasn't a custom in Scotland, at least not yet.

He thought of refraining, so as not to shock the two dozen or so witnesses, but Greyson remembered he'd never see most of them again. So he kissed his wife, fully aware they'd not yet made love. Soon. Hopefully very soon.

"The smile of a man happy with his bride." Ross clapped him on the back as they all left the chapel, heading down the dusty road to the Brennans' manor. "And hopefully not of a marked man with two earls peeved enough to track him down."

Holding Marian's hand, he grimaced at his uncle.

"Thanks for letting us appreciate the moment," he said dryly, but Ross didn't seem overly concerned with his lack of tact.

"When do you leave?"

Ross nodded up ahead to the stables just next to the stone manor. Alban had apparently gone ahead of them and was leading out their mounts even now.

"You don't even want cake?"

Marian watched them, clearly uneasy. He knew she didn't want anyone to fight on her behalf. The violent end of her men had made a mark on her.

"It will be fine," he said with no notion of whether it was true. He looked to Ross to reassure her, and although it took his uncle a while to catch on, he'd give credit where it was due—Ross's tone was most convincing.

"With your dowry and the knowledge we've pieced together, you pieced together, aye lass, your husband has the right of it."

Your husband.

Two words he hadn't thought to hear so soon, but ones that warmed him to his very soul.

"You are certain about this?" Marian asked again.

"Aye, lass," Ross said. "I've met the earl and his son before, and will appeal to them as a fellow ally to Bruce."

They stopped in front of the stables, the cart horse now appearing with her trunks.

"If he does not accept the new terms?"

Ross leaned toward them. "We'll need to find my sister and her other son quickly."

"Us leaving does not help you or your clan."

Grey could tell she was still worried about putting Clan

MacKinnish in a predicament, one with two angry earls on one side and the future king of Scotland's grandfather on the other.

"Bruce may have to be told the truth," Grey said in an undertone, watching Ross mount beside them.

Marian whipped her head toward him.

"You would tell him everything?"

He looked at Ross, who had his own feelings on the matter. There was much still to be discussed, and more they had yet to learn. But given the players involved in the Irvine plot, plus the king's obvious interest in the Bruce, it was seeming more and more likely they would have to bring the man into the fold.

"There are too many uncertainties yet to determine the best path forward," Ross said, preparing to ride out. "But first let me negotiate on your behalf and settle this matter."

Marian looked toward the trunks, then back up to his uncle. Nodding, she thanked him again. With that, Ross and Alban rode off, the cart creaking beneath the weight of Marian's trunks. She'd kept just two gowns. The others were being carted off as a part of her dowry to replace the sole necklace and brooch she'd kept, along with a gold belt and, by her admission, *a few coins.* If their plan succeeded, she wouldn't need more.

"Come inside." Lady Brennan waved them into the manor.

He and Marian followed the others inside, and they were all served cake. Or more precisely, spiced buns piled onto each other in the form of a cake. He thanked Lord and Lady Brennan again for giving them at least some modicum of an actual wedding. Flowers had been brought into the hall, and Greyson couldn't believe how quickly it had been transformed.

Who needed a Degas House wedding when you could be married in a remote manor house in medieval Scotland? Although he did wish they could have a second line, one of New Orleans's famed brass band parades.

For the first time since he'd found himself at Ross's feet in the Cony and Cross, Greyson felt at peace. His wife was by his side, and no one was attempting to murder them at the moment. As soon as Ross returned, they could continue on to Perthshire, where Grey was more and more certain they would find his mother, and possibly Rhys too.

And he could tell she felt the same sense of peace. Her smiles came easily, and they reached her eyes. He'd seen her like this only once before, at Quinting Castle.

"You're watching me."

She took a bite of the cake, and Greyson allowed his gaze to linger on her lips as they closed around her spoon. Jesus. This woman was his wife.

"I am."

"Lady Brennan kindly prepared a private bedchamber," she said.

He liked the way his wife thought. And though he might not know as much as Rhys about the Middle Ages, he did know the consummation of their marriage was more likely to dissuade her betrothed from attempting to reclaim her than the ceremony itself.

Greyson stood, holding out his hand.

"Shall we?"

It didn't take long for the hall to fill with hoots and hollers that could rival the best of any bawdiness New Orleans could offer.

With a nod of thanks to the lord and lady of the manor, Greyson and Marian walked from the hall. Thankfully, no one attempted to follow them. So much for the whole idea of bedding witnesses, one medieval myth that didn't appear to be entirely accurate.

Which was good, because he wasn't prepared to share.

THE HALL HAD BEEN BRIGHT, but not so their bedchamber.

Somehow Marian would find a way to repay the kindness they'd been shown here. Lady Brennan had truly outdone herself.

Though less than half the size of the smallest bedchamber at Fenwall Castle, it was the most magnificent room possible. A fire had been stoked, candles lit. A white canopy hung over their bed as if welcoming them.

"Come here, wife."

Marian laughed as Greyson pulled her toward him the moment he closed the door behind them.

"Do I sound medieval enough?"

Greyson's hands wound through the hair at the nape of her neck.

"I've not heard anyone speak like that, but I have also never been a wife before."

"Hmmm." That sound, deep in his throat . . .

When Greyson's lips descended onto hers, Marian was immediately lost. But not the kind of lost she'd felt after leaving

Fenwall behind, knowing she would likely never return. This was a glorious, welcome kind of feeling. All but him fell away.

All but the touch of his lips.

She'd tried to imagine her wedding night, or day as it happened, but the sensation of air on her bare skin, Greyson's lips on her neck . . . never could she have imagined such an exquisite pleasure.

"I wanted to take it slow."

His words were at odds with his actions, but Marian encouraged it. She helped him, in fact, until each piece of her clothing, and his, lay at their feet.

She stared, unable to look away.

"Are you scared?" he asked, watching her.

"I've not seen . . . that is to say . . ." Marian concentrated on his chest instead. The markings, tattoos he'd called them. They had fascinated her before, but they were even more enticing now, each and every one on display.

"You're so goddamn beautiful."

Marian allowed Greyson to lead her to the bed. Aye, she was nervous. She'd not felt anything other than excitement all morn, but now, unsure of what to expect . . .

"Let me tell you what will happen here."

Lying down with Greyson moving atop her, Marian swallowed.

"I will kiss every inch of you first."

He began straightaway. First, her lips. Then her neck. Bringing her hands up to his shoulders, pressing him closer, she gave over to the feelings and attempted to forget what was to come. Gilda had told Marian of her duties to Duncan, but they'd hardly sounded pleasant.

Greyson, however . . .

Every bit of what he did to her was very pleasant. Surely that would be no different.

"And then," he murmured, his lips wrapping around her

nipple, "I will prepare you, my lovely Maid Marian."

"Prepare me?"

Light flickered off the canopy above them as Marian let Greyson guide her knees open.

Holding himself over her with one hand, he used the other to stroke her hips and then the inside of her thigh.

"Wider."

When she did his bidding, his fingers entered her, ever so slowly. As she became accustomed to it, Greyson increased the pressure. His thumb teased as she tried, unsuccessfully, to get a better grip on his shoulders.

Giving up and clutching the coverlet beneath her instead, Marian abandoned each and every one of Gilda's well-meaning comments about the marriage bed. Because this was no duty. What Greyson was doing to her just now . . .

"And then, only when you're ready—" Her eyes popped open. Marian wasn't even aware she'd closed them. "—I will make you mine."

Guiding himself toward her, Greyson did not take his eyes from hers.

"It will hurt, but hopefully just for a few seconds."

He was inside her.

"Hopefully?"

Filling her, little by little.

"I'm not in the habit of bedding virgins."

Until . . .

"Hold on to me."

She'd barely brought her hands up when a sharp pain had her clutching at him like a wounded cat, clawing at his back, attempting to shut out the sting of it.

"I am so sorry."

This kiss was soft, tender. But as the pain subsided, it became more like his others: all-consuming.

It surprised her when she found her own hips lifting to meet his. He moved more quickly only when she did, the pace set by her.

And Marian suddenly wanted more. Much, much more.

"It doesn't hurt anymore."

Hands on each side of her, the muscles in Greyson's arms flexed with every thrust. She couldn't decide if they, or the look on his face, were more pleasurable to look at.

When he lowered himself, his chest touching hers, that same urgency from before took over. Every bit of Marian tensed. She met each thrust, encouraging them even.

"Marian . . ."

His face, she decided—that's what she liked to look at most. The love in his eyes as he reached down between them and, with one touch, sent her spiraling into oblivion. The last thing she was aware of Greyson's moan of pleasure as he tossed his head back and thrust one final time.

The world slipped away, leaving just the two of them, his arms around her, his body's shudders mirroring her own. Everything was sensation.

They lay there, Marian content to say nothing.

When he pulled from her, the loss was only momentary as he kissed her so gently every doubt she'd ever had melted away.

"Next, we will wash"—he propped himself back up and nodded to the bowl of rose water beside their bed—"drink some wine, and do that all over again.

Marian smiled. "I like your accounting of that."

"A play-by-play," he teased, though Marian had no idea what that meant.

He pushed up to sit beside her. "So much to teach you," he said, "in bed, and out of it."

"Someday I will need to learn more of your customs." Marian lifted herself onto her elbows. "But we are still in my time, and 'tis you who are the student."

"Is that right?" he asked with a grin.

"Aye, 'tis so."

"Mayhap tomorrow we shall begin your lessons, Maid Marian. This day belongs to the pleasures that can be wrought between a man and a woman."

Marian burst out laughing. His words. His accent.

He sounded very much like a Scotsman.

Her Scotsman.

She would emulate his speech, repeating something she'd heard him say once before.

"Let the games begin."

"Nay," Marian told him, "we do not believe the world to be flat."

They sat in front of the fire, clothed for the first time in days. As far as honeymoons went, this tiny village, not much bigger than a hamlet except that it had a chapel—a rarity, according to Marian—was better than sitting on a beach in the Caribbean. Or skiing in Aspen, his father's favorite vacation.

Eating freshly baked bread, drinking ale with lunch and hardly leaving a room that could easily pass for a medieval-style B&B back home . . . all of it had been idyllic.

Especially given the woman with whom he shared it.

Greyson could tell she was worried about his uncle. About Duncan and her father. And so was he. But he was so enjoying this time with Marian, this respite from the constant fighting and stress, having the opportunity to train and talk with his clansmen, that he didn't wish for Ross to rush back.

He took another sip of wine, grateful Marian had kept some of her coin so she could offer compensation to Lord and Lady Brennan. Comfortable as they might be here, it was obvious he'd been wrong about another facet of medieval life.

Titled did not mean rich.

He tried again.

"Are chastity belts really a thing?"

She had no clue what he meant.

"You know. A belt that locks up your hoo-ha."

"My what?" Marian laughed as he pointed to show her. "Oh, Grey, you are mad. 'Tis your turn." She lifted her goblet. "What do you drink in your time?"

"You'll be happy to learn we drink wine that tastes much like this. But the ale—beer we call it—is completely different."

"Will I like it? Your time?"

They'd talked many times over the last few days about what would happen when they found his mother, his brother, and the cross that had obviously been used to pull his mom back. Pretending it would be as easy as walking from St. Louis Cathedral to Cafe du Monde, they operated under the assumption that they would indeed make it back.

An assumption Greyson knew was quite a leap.

"You will," he said, more confidently than he felt. "Once we find my mother, she can tell you, us, about the adjustment."

Just imagining his mother being transported, alone, from this place and time to New Orleans . . . he shut the thought from his mind. It was too horrible to consider. He and Rhys had at least known what they were getting themselves into. Even if they had not quite believed it.

"Do you think—"

A knock at their door interrupted her.

Marian bolted up, likely sharing his thought: Ross was due back any day. When she opened the door, a chambermaid stood there.

"Pardon, my lady. But a guest has arrived. Master Ross wishes to speak with you both."

Marian thanked her and shut the door. Before he could say a word, she put her goblet down and started dressing, the under-tunic and kirtle she'd worn the day they met on in no time.

With luck, he'd be able to take it back off just as quickly.

When they were both ready, Marian pulled the iron handle on the door, but Greyson stopped her.

"No matter what he says, know we are in this together. Wife."

Greyson drew his brows together in mock concentration. She'd explained the difference between a medieval man and a caveman, of course, but he still liked to tease her.

Marian stood on her toes, kissed him, and then pulled open the door.

"Aye, husband. I know as much."

He smiled all the way to the hall, but his smile fled the moment he saw Ross's face. The cavernous space was empty except for Ross and a handful of servants, bathed in an eerie glow from only a half dozen wall torches. The sight sent a rash of goose bumps along Greyson's arms.

How easy it was to forget, this was no bed-and-breakfast.

Their honeymoon had come at the expense of breaking a marriage agreement between two earls. Something, he'd come to learn, that was not so easily done.

Insomuch as Greyson had ever thought of earls prior to coming here, he'd thought they were a little like knights, that they were pretty much everywhere. Not so, he'd learned. With less than two dozen in each country, the power of a man like Marian's father put his own family's influence to shame.

"Ross," he said, sitting across from him at the trestle table.

A servant had brought his uncle a bowl of stew and a tankard of ale. The man offered to bring them refreshment as well, but Greyson sent him away as Marian settled on the bench.

"Where's Alban?"

"Stables."

Greyson moved Marian's hand to his leg and covered it with

his own—a silent assurance that they would overcome this. Whatever this was.

"What news?"

Ross finished chewing, but the servant returned with a cloth before he could speak. Another medieval misconception. More people used handkerchiefs in this time than his own.

Greyson and Marian exchanged a somewhat frustrated glance. He was trying to conceal his worry, but he doubted he was succeeding. Had he ever felt this wound up in a board meeting?

Ross grunted, then said, "Your betrothed is even more of an arse than rumored."

"Former betrothed," Greyson pointed out.

"You met him?" Marian asked. "What did his father say?"

The servant had finally moved away. When Ross leaned forward, as if about to relate a secret, Greyson caught the flash of defiance in his eyes. It was a look he'd seen often enough on his mother.

"All is well." Greyson said it unthinkingly, but he felt sure of it.

Though he could have dispelled their concerns earlier, Ross finally smiled. "Aye."

His shoulders sagged with relief. "What's with the dramatics?"

Ross and Marian gave him *that* look.

"Why not say so earlier?" he tried again. "And why do you look like you're about to murder someone?"

His uncle, the Viking, grunted.

"The food in Pittillock is shite. We stayed on the road on our return." He took another bite of stew.

Apparently being hangry was another trait his uncle and his mother had in common.

"The earl took my dowry?" Marian shifted even closer to him. He could feel her body heat, could sense her unease.

Rubbing his hand across her thigh, he waited for his uncle's response.

"He did. And was none too pleased at the prospect of being manipulated by your father. You're a lucky lass to be rid of such a man."

Marian tensed.

Her father was not a good man, or at least he hadn't been one to her. But still, he was the only parent she'd ever known, and she'd always been reluctant to speak out against him. Greyson tried to understand, but since he wanted nothing more than to punch the asshole in the face, he had a hard time reconciling her conflicted feelings toward him.

So instead, he remained silent, not feeling the need to give an unsolicited opinion.

"He believed you, then?" she asked.

Ross frowned. Clearly it hadn't been as easy as that.

"After a bit of blustering, aye, he believed me. It seems, though ill-timed, Bruce's invasion of Balliol served as a reminder to all. The Maid of Norway is but a babe. The Guardians, Fife included, have their doubts about the stability of the current arrangement. Even as an ally to Bruce, Fife admitted the man was sending a clear signal to King Edward. Bruce will do what is necessary to defeat his rivals."

"So he agreed King Edward is positioning himself for the throne?"

Ross shook his head. "Only the three of us know that to be true. With Greyson's perspective, 'tis easy to see. But there is enough mistrust of the English king on this side of the border that even a hint of his treachery is enough to turn the tide. I could not ascertain for certain his complicity in balancing his Scottish and English interests, but I assured him the king was looking for a way to gain influence, if not control."

It seemed too easy.

"And the gold helped matters. Apparently Fife cares more

about filling his coffers than he does about gaining a question-able ally."

Ross downed the rest of his ale in one swig.

"He blustered until I offered him the coin."

"So 'tis done?"

Brodie walked into the hall then. It was too bad he hadn't been with Ross from the start. Unlike his usually surly uncle, Brodie smiled like a man who had just returned from averting a crisis. One look at him would have reassured them of the outcome.

"'Tis done," Ross agreed. "And now, my boy." He slammed the table so hard an observer might think him angry, but Greyson knew the Viking better now. "We go home."

3 0

Ross helped her dismount, the break a much needed one. After five days in the saddle with little rest, Marian had begun to feel the effects.

"No tarrying," Ross called to them as they left the side of the road to find a private spot for her. If time travel was possible, perhaps reincarnation was also real. If so, she wondered what it might be like to return as a man. No need to scour the woods looking for a place to squat.

"What are you smiling about?"

She found a spot and hurried ahead. "Just wondering what it might be like to be a man," she said, indicating for Grey to stay behind the bush. How odd that she should still feel so shy with him. In the past days, she'd laid everything bare to him. Her body, most especially.

Marian grinned, thinking about the nights since their wedding. Grey had promised to be a dutiful, and thorough, instructor. And he had indeed. She finished, righted her kirtle, and returned to her husband.

"Have you ever wondered what it would be like to be a woman?"

She thought to make their way back to the others, but apparently Grey had other plans. He pulled her toward him, his kiss unhurried. She returned the affection gladly, meeting each thrust of his tongue and forgetting everything but the two of them for a moment.

Grey's groan reminded her the kiss would go no further. Not now. But he didn't let her go just yet.

"God, no. And have to wipe myself with a leaf, hoping it's not poison ivy?" His eyes widened. "Do you have poison ivy here?"

She shook her head. "Poison ivy?"

"A plant. Makes you itchy and blistery."

That did indeed sound unpleasant.

"Before they tore it out, my brother Reikart fell into an ivy plant one night in Larkin Park. We live in a place called Algiers Point, just across the river from our office and the rest of the family in the Quarter."

"The French Quarter?"

"Yep, you've got it. By the time we get back it'll be like you know the place already."

A sliver of foreboding tugged at her, as it always did during these types of discussions, but she shoved it away. She liked his optimism. She truly wanted to believe it would be that easy.

"You're worried." Still holding her, Grey didn't seem inclined to let go. And Marian wasn't going to be the one to do it. She could happily stand here, with him, all day.

"What if—"

"Nope. Not gonna do it. We have to stay positive. Think only good thoughts."

"But is that not courting disaster?" she asked, speaking words that had been spoken to her more than once, mostly by her father. "Certainly not all those good thoughts will end in good outcomes."

"If they don't, we'll deal with them then." Grey pointed to

her head. "Wait until you learn about neurology. Brain science has always fascinated me."

"Neurology?" The word felt awkward on her lips.

"The study of the brain. For instance, they've learned positive thinking actually improves your ability to think and analyze. Which means you can affect your own outcomes sometimes by the way you think about a challenge."

Sometimes it was truly difficult to grasp the concepts Grey attempted to explain. Neurology. How could one go about studying the brain without killing the subject?

"So, the day we met. I may not have hidden in the woods, crippled by indecision, had I believed I could get away?"

Grey smiled. "Perhaps. But then I wouldn't have had the chance to hold you."

"That day we stood in the woods, you held me as a stranger. Today, you do so as my husband." A word she still liked repeating, much like she enjoyed being called his wife.

"One who values his life, which Ross will likely take if we don't return soon."

She'd been thinking the same thing. Reluctantly, after one more quick kiss, Grey dropped his arms, taking her hand instead. As predicted, Ross was not particularly happy about their delay.

"It was quicker traveling with a cart horse than a couple newly married."

"Is he always such a cranky old man?" Grey asked Alban, who'd mounted just next to them.

"Ye know the answer to that already."

The others laughed, all except for Ross himself.

The exchange, though of no particular import, was one Marian continued to consider as they rode the final leg of their journey.

Grey had obviously formed a tight bond with his uncle. His clan. Would he find it hard to leave them? Even Marian would miss the men who had quickly become like family to her. What Ross had done, the risk he had taken for them . . . she could never hope to repay him. Marian would try by offering him the largest jewel she'd taken from her trunk, an enormous ruby that was rumored to have been given to her grandfather by the King of France.

Getting the stubborn man to take it would be another challenge, but Marian was determined.

"There it is," Ross said some time later, pointing at an edifice in the distance.

The sun had set not long before, leaving enough light to clearly illuminate the outline of Castle Hightower. The name, apt. It rose before them, surrounded by rolling hills, a majestic beacon for their weary group. She glanced at Grey.

He stared up at it, mouth open, as if this were his first day in the past. Marian herself shivered at his expression.

Would his mother be there? What about his brother? Marian had prayed many times for it to be so, and now it seemed they would learn if her prayers would be answered.

His mother's home.

Castle Hightower was built in 1201 by the first laird of the MacKinnish clan. The castle is best known as one of the places Robert the Bruce was hidden when he was first crowned king of Scotland and King Edward of England was hunting him. It is said that Castle Hightower burned to the ground in 1306, and that the MacKinnish laird was hanged for his part in aiding Robert the Bruce.

It was something Rhys had read to him sometime in his last feverish days in his own time. How the hell had he forgotten? It was as if the words had soaked into his brain without surfacing until this moment.

The laird and his son. His mother must know too. She'd have done the research.

Was it Ross? Another of his uncles he'd not yet met?

Greyson took a deep breath.

Rising from the earth, three towers surrounded by lush countryside that would make the family gardener weep, Castle Hightower stood before them. As they approached, a horn blew to announce their arrival.

He'd never seen anything more beautiful, save Marian's face next to him as he woke up each morning. Fanciful, his brothers had always called him, and maybe he was, but this looked like something from a fantasy movie. The fact that his aunt Grace apparently had fae friends only added to the image.

Heart hammering as they approached the courtyard filled with people, he felt as if he were returning home after a long journey. The feeling was so strong he could be pulling onto St. Charles Avenue.

And then he saw her.

Greyson could no more stop his reaction than he could have stopped loving Marian just because she was promised to another. Tears flowed for the first time since he'd seen his father lying in that hospital room. Which had only been the second time he could recall crying as an adult.

The first had been when this beautiful, radiant woman had disappeared from his life.

"Grey!"

Cheeks streaked with tears, just as his were, Greyson's mother, appearing just as she had when she disappeared five years ago, enveloped him. Her arms were like a winter jacket on a frigid day in the north.

The American north. Lord knew what winter was like here in Scotland.

"Son," she whispered into his ear, her tears wet against his cheek. "I love you. I missed you so much."

"You're alive. Oh my God, Mom. You're here."

He tried not to let anyone else hear him. Greyson had no idea who knew, and who did not.

He was mumbling, making no sense. How would they explain this reunion?

He squeezed her again and then reluctantly pulled back.

"Rhys?"

Her smile answered him before she spoke. His brother was alive! "He's not here now." Greyson sucked in a breath.

"Shhh, it's okay. He's fine. Just not at Hightower at the moment."

He's fine.

Rhys was here. Alive. And he was fine.

"What about Reikart?" she asked. "And Ian? Did they come through with you?"

"No. Nothing. We tried to make it through together, but I think I'm the only one who did. If they're here, I haven't seen or heard anything of them."

They were still home. They had to be. Greyson could hardly breathe. It took every bit of self-control he had to pretend he was fine.

"It's okay, Grey. It will be okay."

Aye, it would. His mother and brother were alive.

"Mom"—he looked around them—"how will we explain?"

Wiping his cheek with the back of her sleeve, as if he were five, his mother smiled.

"Let me worry about that."

She peered over his shoulder. Marian had dismounted.

He let go of his mother and reached for her.

"Let me guess," his mom said as he pulled Marian toward them. "Your wife?"

Nothing she could have said would have surprised him more.

"What would make you say that?" He wasn't typically the

commitment type, never mind the marrying one.

"It seems bringing wives home to Hightower is the new McCaim tradition."

Did that mean . . .

"Your brother Rhys. He's married as well."

He nearly said, *Shut the fuck up*. Thank the Lord he caught himself. Cursing in front of his mother was a no-go. But Rhys? Married? The same guy who turned tail and ran when any woman asked for more than his first name? Hard to believe.

"He arrived two months ago with her, but they've gone to take back Maggie's inheritance. A long story . . ."

She turned to Marian, who bowed. Like an earl's daughter.

This was surreal.

"Lady Marian of Fenwall, my wife. Marian, this is my mother, Shona MacKinnish."

"Pleased to finally meet you," Marian said, but then his mother bowed too.

"Lady Marian."

If he lived here the rest of his life, he would never figure out which titles trumped each other, who you bowed to and who you didn't. And he'd thought the etiquette of handshakes and twenty-first-century greetings were complicated.

"Fenwall, as in the Earl of Fenwall along the border?" his mother asked.

"Aye, my lady. The earl is my father."

"Another long story," Grey added. "But I can feel a big, hulking Viking presence behind me."

"Viking?" His mother laughed, embracing her brother. "Ross is no Viking. But I would like to hear how you two ended up together. We'd heard rumors of it, that you traveled together. I'd wanted to believe them so badly."

Ross grinned and whispered for the four of them only to hear. "Your son appeared at my feet. Some in this family know proper reverence at least."

Shona rolled her eyes. "I revere you above all others, Ross," she teased.

He cleared his throat. "Even Alastair?"

"Definitely Alastair."

"You only say that because he's not here. Where is he?"

"Hunting with our father."

"And the others?"

"All gone. Some with Rhys, some to Bruce. But everyone is safe," she reassured him.

Greyson couldn't take his eyes off her, still stunned that his mother was here, standing in front of him. The shock of it hadn't worn off.

"For now, we've much to discuss," Ross said.

The understatement of the year.

"Come inside. And welcome to the family," his mother said to Marian and then turned to him. "Grey. Welcome home. To your other home."

For now, this one would have to be enough.

EPILOGUE

"Stirling Castle." Greyson whistled as they rode up the hill toward the castle. "It's crazy to think about the things that will happen here."

With only Marian and Brodie nearby, he was free to talk openly. They'd finally let Brodie in on their secret.

"In less than five years, it will be under English control again." Something his mother had told him before they left Hightower.

"Your mother said it will change hands five times before the boy takes it back," Marian said.

The only people who knew the truth at Highwater were the immediate family and those who'd known Shona before her journey. They'd learned to talk in code to avoid revealing their secret. "The boy" was twelve-year-old Bruce, the one who would one day be king.

"I knew I'd heard of it before. That bridge"—he pointed to the one they'd crossed earlier—"will go down in history for its role in the Battle of Stirling Bridge. Everyone will know William Wallace, even in my country."

In the month since they'd returned to Hightower, his

mother, his grandfather, and Ross had all agreed changing history was a dangerous undertaking, but they were determined to at least make the Bruce understand the situation as it stood. If he thought King Edward a possible ally, they aimed to change his mind. Make the grandfather and the son understand the English king's motives were not, would never be, pure. When it came to the Scottish crown, Edward cared little for mediation.

He planned to take what he wanted for himself.

They were here to guide the Bruce. It would be great if Greyson could simply walk up to the man and tell him everything he knew, but everyone knew it wasn't so simple. Besides, they still had work to do. They needed to expose Baron Bellecote, the baron who'd schemed with Edward to see Alexander murdered. Apparently Rhys's new wife had been betrothed to marry the bastard.

And they had one more goal: to find Grace and the cross and get the hell home.

"Will ye talk to the Bruce yerself, or leave Ross to it?" Brodie asked.

Apparently Greyson's speech wasn't quite up to snuff. His "speak like a medieval Scot" lessons with Marian inevitably turned into a very different kind of lessons each night. His mother tried, but apparently it wasn't so easy to transcend seven hundred years in a few short months.

"Ross will do the talking, but I damn sure plan to be there."

"You are certain it's wise, Grey?" Marian asked. Neither she nor his mother thought it was a good idea for him to take part. But he'd decided he couldn't just sit around and wait, no matter how compelling his wife's company.

His mother had remained at Hightower. Someone needed to be there who knew everything that was happening. Especially since there was still a chance one of his other brothers might show up. They knew about Hightower Castle. If they ended up in this time, they'd rendezvous there.

"I'm certain," he said with as much authority as possible.

But Marian could see right through him, something she excelled at.

"You're nervous."

He loved when she talked twenty-first century like that.

Greyson could see Brodie watching him as they approached the others, who'd stopped at the gatehouse.

"No. Not at all," he lied.

Nervous about meeting the man who held his clan's allegiance? About chitchatting with a boy who would someday become the King of Scotland? What was there to be nervous about? He did this kind of thing all the time.

"You have that smile," Marian said. "Do I want to know what you're thinking?"

"Nay, my lady. You do not."

Brodie rolled his eyes as Uncle Ross talked to the guards. Eventually, their party was let inside, but it would be some time before they actually reached the keep. That was another thing that continued to surprise him. It was like being in Las Vegas. The buildings were so big they looked like they were right down the street, but really they were miles away.

These castles, Stirling in particular, were absolutely sprawling.

But before long, they were being led into the massive front doors of the main keep. Just before they entered, he watched as Marian pulled her mantle closed. For someone who'd been raised in Northern England, she had a remarkable dislike of the cold.

Greyson couldn't wait to get her to New Orleans.

"That smile again."

As they were greeted by the steward, he fought the urge to grab her. Kiss the hell out of her. He was learning, ever a dutiful student. Public displays of affection always brought strange looks. Which was fine at Hightower, where everyone knew him as the eccentric relative from the south.

But Greyson couldn't bring that kind of attention to them here. He had come as a passive observer. And, oddly enough, he was fine with that fact.

He had nothing to prove. Not to Marian or his uncle, not even to himself.

The fact that they'd entered a royal residence was evident everywhere.

"Jesus," he whispered to Marian, "I thought Quinting was impressive."

To think the English called their northern neighbors heathens. The décor was just as colorful, but there was gold everywhere, on everything.

"Remarkable given how often it's been ravaged," she whispered back.

When Marian leaned this close to him, he risked being the uncouth American who whisked his wife into his arms and embarrassed them both. That smell, uniquely hers, was created for him alone.

Greyson was convinced fate had brought them together. His mother had said more times than he could count that this wasn't the son she knew. But it wasn't the five years apart that had made the change. It was just Greyson 2.0. Post time travel. Post Marian.

"You think we're likely to get a private bedchamber?"

The steward ordered a servant to take their belongings. Apparently they'd be meeting the Bruce family sooner rather than later.

"This way. My lord has been waiting for you," the steward said to Ross.

Looking at him and Marian, the steward paused. "My lady? I shall have you accompanied to the hall with the others."

Apparently only he and Ross were allowed into the solar chamber.

Fuck that.

"Lady Marian of Fenwall," he introduced his wife, "will be accompanying us."

He could establish rank with the best of them. And thankfully, the steward didn't bat an eye. Not so Ross, who openly glared at him.

Greyson gave his uncle a look back but mouthed, *okay*. He knew his place. Kind of.

In contrast to the glitz of the great hall, the men inside the solar looked every bit as ordinary as he and his uncle. As they were introduced, Greyson realized the elder Bruce, the grandfather, wasn't in attendance.

But his son and grandson were, and Greyson couldn't stop staring. This boy would be king.

Their demeanor as casual as their dress, Lord Bruce grasped his uncle's shoulder like he was an old college roommate.

"So a relative, aye?"

Bruce was looking at him.

"Greyson McCaim and his wife, Lady Marian."

"Fenwall's daughter," Bruce interjected, gesturing for them all to sit. For a solar, the chamber was dark as shit. If they had to stay in this time, Greyson would become a damn candlemaker. They'd for sure never go out of business.

"Well informed, as always," Ross said, sitting next to him on the medieval equivalent of a loveseat with more intricately embroidered cushions than a wrought iron railing in the Quarter.

"Her father isn't pleased."

Marian stiffened.

"But apparently has accepted the fact that his alliance to us will be through Clan MacKinnish instead of Fife."

Greyson winced. This guy pretty much knew everything already.

Well, except for all the future-based information they had to share.

"Her dowry," Ross said, his tone slightly defensive, "without any nuptials, is more goodwill than Fife deserved."

Damn. His uncle wasn't here to mince words.

"Perhaps. But your loyalty," Bruce said, just as directly, "is to Clan Bruce."

"My lord," Marian cut in. "I do apologize if my altered wedding plans have caused the Bruce family any distress. Please know, Clan MacKinnish is as devoted to you as any ally has ever been to my father, if not more so. As for my father's distress . . ."

They all watched as Marian seemed to struggle to find the words.

"It matters not," she continued.

Well then.

"His loyalty lies with King Edward, and him alone. I can attest personally to the fact."

Bruce stared at his wife for a little too long. But not in that way. Ross had told him the man had actually married for love, a fact that wasn't lost on any of them.

Not that they were relying on his sense of romanticism to buy them goodwill and an ear inclined to listen. But still.

"'You fell in love with my flowers and not my roots. So when autumn came, you knew not what to do.'"

They all turned to look at the boy who stood behind his father.

"Robert." His father's word was a warning.

But as Lord Bruce and Ross continued to talk, Greyson could not help but watch the boy. They'd dismissed him out of hand. But his words . . . he had no idea where they came from, or who the boy had quoted, but they told Greyson one thing.

He already knew.

Somehow, he knew what his elders did not, at least not yet. Maybe he had the advantage of being quieted too often, something that had given him the opportunity to listen more.

But at least one person in this chamber suspected what they already knew to be true. King Edward was not to be trusted.

"What are your thoughts on the matter?" Lord Bruce's words to Greyson pulled him out of his thoughts.

Somehow Ross had navigated the discussion to exactly where they'd wanted it. No big revelations, just planting a seed for now. Once they had more details about Bellecote and the Irvines, the Bruce family would be told more, maybe even all of it.

For now, he smiled at the future king. "I believe, as Master Bruce suggests, that there is something to be learned from the English king."

If his answer was deliberately vague, he'd done his job. It seemed to satisfy Lord Bruce, but not the boy. He peered at him as if trying to figure out what, exactly, was to be learned from King Edward.

Future Earl of Carrick, hold on to your convictions. Accept the English king as an ally against the Johns, Balliol and Comyn. When Comyn seizes your estates, accept Edward's aid then too. But when he attacks your own people, it will be time to turn on him.

And you'll do it.

Of course, he couldn't say any of it out loud. But as the two of them continued their staring contest, Greyson fancied the boy somehow understood him.

Fancied.

Jesus, he needed to get back to the twenty-first century.

"You'll stay at Stirling for a sennight at least," Lord Bruce was saying now.

Never more grateful for a meeting to be over, Greyson stood with the others.

"A few days," his uncle said. "You'll tell me what's happened since Turnberry?"

"Aye." Bruce nodded his head to him and Marian. "Your chambers are prepared. Allow the Bruce hospitality to welcome you both to our cause."

Yep. So he was pretty much officially a supporter of Clan Bruce and their campaign to take the Scottish throne. It would be pretty cool if Greyson hadn't known it would take them twenty years to come out ahead. And if he had any clue whether or not Reikart and Ian figured out how to properly say the chant, coming through time after him.

Finding his brothers across seven hundred years might prove more difficult than being smack-dab in the middle of a medieval history lesson.

"Many thanks, Lord Bruce," Marian said. Greyson echoed her words and left with a final glance at the boy. As their group walked toward the great hall, he looked at Ross, who nodded. The Viking was back. Anytime Ross wanted to make an impression, he scowled like that.

Maybe Greyson should try that tactic in the boardroom.

"Will you pardon us, Ross?" Marian asked suddenly. "We will join you in the hall soon."

Ross grunted and walked away, but not before Greyson caught the hint of a smile.

"Our chamber, if it pleases you," Marian said to one of the two servants who'd accompanied them from the solar.

"Aye, my lady."

And he felt another surge of love for his wife—a nearly constant sensation, truth be told.

She had literally just skipped out on the midday meal for an afternoon "lesson." Because there was no doubt from the look in her eyes what this was all about.

Greyson confirmed it the minute he closed the chamber door behind him.

He didn't say a word, and neither did she.

Instead, he kissed her, hard. Remembering she wouldn't have more than one change of clothes, he was as careful as possible when removing them. Not that he was a caveman who'd tear off his wife's clothing in an effort to have sex with her.

A medieval man, maybe, but not a Neanderthal.

"Here?" Marian asked when he pushed her naked body up against the door. The bed was too damn far away.

"Aye, here."

She wrapped her legs around his waist when he lifted her, but it was up to him to guide himself inside, and Greyson did precisely that.

"Mmmm," was the last thing he heard as he captured her lips once again. Marian set the pace as he held her up, his arms straightening as he indulged in the glorious delight of being inside his wife. Unfortunately, with his hands holding her up, he couldn't caress her everywhere. Maybe later. They would take it slow, Greyson continuing to explore every curve.

This was not the time for slow sensual pleasures, but for raw, unchecked passion. When she stilled, clenching around him, Greyson all but roared with pleasure pumping through him one last time.

Still for a moment, he finally, reluctantly, let her down. But he didn't let her go.

Greyson would never let her go.

"Well, Maid Marian, it seems your lesson on afternoon delights is complete."

He kissed her nose and tried to smooth down her hair, knowing they'd have to return to the hall.

"I should think so. After all, who better to teach me than my very own"—she stood on her tiptoes and kissed him back—"Robin Hood."

Laughing at her own joke, Marian broke away and reached

down for her kirtle. Greyson took the opportunity she offered and slapped her glorious ass.

"Oh!"

She stood back up, smiling.

"Lest you forget, wife, Robin was, first and foremost, an outlaw. A man who abided by no one's rules but his own."

Marian raised her brows.

"OK, and maybe by Maid Marian's too. I am, after all, a *modern* medieval man."

For now

REIKART MCCAIN IS NEXT. CONTINUE HIGHLANDER'S THROUGH TIME BOOK THREE WITH SEDUCTIVE SCOT. . .

Cecelia Mecca is the author of medieval romance, including the Border Series, and sometimes wishes she could be transported back in time to the days of knights and castles. Although the former English teacher's actual home is in Northeast Pennsylvania where she lives with her husband and two children, her online home can be found at CeceliaMecca.com. She would love to hear from you.

If you'd prefer to chat with one of Cecelia's characters instead, Greyson McCaim is waiting to talk to you about his series, a brand new Scottish time travel called Highlander's Through Time. Subscribe to chat with Grey here.

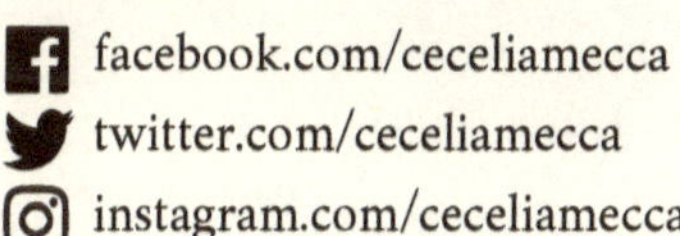